JUDGED, THE SERIES
ALI PARKER

♡ Emily!

This is one of my all-time favorites. Enjoy ♡

Ali Parker

Also by Ali Parker

Baited

Second Chance Romances

Jaded

Justified

Judged

Alpha Billionaire Series

His Needs

His Rules

His Way

His Place

His Demands

His Mark

His Offer

His Forever

Together Forever

Bad Money Series

Blood Money

Dirty Money

Forbidden Fruit Series

Forgotten Bodyguard

First Edition.

Editor: Nicole Bailey, Proof Before You Publish & CJ Pinard

Cover Art: Kellie Dennis at Book Cover by Design

A past filled with harmful teasing isn't easily overcome. Neither is a history of crime and death.

Once judged, always judged.

Sicily Moretti comes from a long line of good cooking and large hips. Having graduated at the top of her class from the Culinary Institute of America, she finds success in sugary treats and rich pastries. Having moved from New York to Maine with her closest friend, Kari and Lisa, she's looking for a new start where the building of her own bakery will be her focus. She's not looking for love, nor is she interested in it. She's been judged incorrectly too many times.

Drake DeMarco comes from a long line of crime, his new life a fresh start. His older, Demetri worked hard to help the feisty alpha male cut ties with who he was born to be, his past completely hidden to everyone in the small town of Bar Harbor. He's invested in the town's only gym and is working hard to keep his attention only on his business, but everything changes when a dark-haired beauty begins to steal not only his attention, but his heart.

With a past that would land him in jail, he's beyond scared to let Sicily in. Good thing she doesn't seem in the least bit interested. Will he finally push past his fear of having her judge his family and their nefarious ways and force her to see him for who he is on the inside?

The past follows them until they turn and face it, reconciling who they once were from who they are to become - together.

Table of Contents

CHAPTER ONE

Sicily pressed her forehead to the door of the dressing room and let out a long sigh. Was there anything more depressing than trying on clothes because you couldn't fit into a damn thing in your closet?

"You okay?" Kari's voice was far too soft, her friend aware of her struggles.

"I guess. I just think this is stupid. I plan on losing this extra weight... like now. Spending money I really don't have on clothes that I'm not going to be able to wear soon seems dumb." Sicily moved back and unzipped the pants that fit perfectly. Too bad they were two sizes bigger than she wore back in New York. It had been six months since she, Lisa and Kari had left New York and moved to Bar Harbor, Maine. The need to break away from the big city and start a new life had panned out well for both Kari and Lisa, each of them in happy, healthy relationships.

I'm the only one without a guy. Maybe if I was thinner... Definitely.

"Sicily. Losing weight is a great plan, but you have to have something covering your pretty butt now or you're going to give all these older people a heart attack." Kari let out a short laugh and Sicily forced herself to chuckle as well.

The community was more of a retirement locale, but there were still plenty of people their age working and living around them. It wasn't about wanting someone to make her feel pretty or keep her company, but more about fitting in. Being the fifth wheel with her friends was getting old. She would start looking for love as soon as she got back into shape. No one deserved to be with someone who was obsessive about her size and most likely headed toward a heart attack any minute.

She shuddered at the thought, pushing down the memories of her mother's death earlier that year.

"Do those pants fit? They were cute." Kari's voice was hopeful, leaving Sicily to feel like shit that she hadn't told Kari no to her coming. It was traumatizing enough to realize that she needed to step on the scale, seeing that she had gained more weight than she had convinced herself of. Having her best friend, her thin, beautiful, best friend, standing on the other side of the door trying to coach and encourage her was mortifying.

Sicily took a slow breath and turned to look in the mirror as tears burned her gaze. "I'm good."

"No you're not. I can hear it."

"I just need a few minutes. I'll meet you up front." Sicily swallowed the thick knot that sat in her throat.

Moving back to the small bench in the room, she sunk down on it and pressed her hands to her knees, trying to force herself to pull it together. It was just a few pounds. She would go for a jog that afternoon and start back on her meat and veggies diet at lunch. Owning the best bakery in Bar Harbor didn't mean she had to look the part of a trustworthy chef.

Maybe if she had decided to sell diet products or to bake pastries and treats without sugar or flour or oil. She rolled her eyes and slid her hands into her long dark hair, tugging a little in hopes of letting out a little bit of her angst. How long had she watched her weight to make sure she didn't look like her mother's side of the family? They were Sicilian and her mother and older brother were far too heavy, their legs thin and middles portly.

"And she died because of it. You will too. Fat ass." Sicily glanced up at herself in the mirror, flinching at the harshness of her own words. Being the only one in the room when her mother suffered a massive heart attack had left a severe toll on her and yet here she was... starting to look more and more like the woman she missed every day since her passing.

Sicily angrily wiped her tears away and got up, tugging the pants off and leaving her back to the mirror. She didn't want to see herself without clothes covering up most of her. It was mid-October and she was so beyond grateful for fall's arrival. Not because of the cooler weather or all of the great events and holidays. It was simply a time where she could wear jeans and sweaters and cover herself up without looking ridiculous. Everyone would be joining her in the comfort of fall attire. Shorts and tank tops and bathing suits be damned.

She checked her face once before walking out of the dressing room, the puffiness around her chestnut gaze leaving it more than obvious that she had wept in the small room and had far too many issues. She paused by the front counter as a thin older woman glanced up.

"Is this all for you dear?"

Sicily kept her head down, making like she was trying to find her card in her purse. She was grateful that Kari was near the front, moving through the racks. Her friend would know right away that she was struggling, and in her kindness would cause Sicily to lose the composure she was tightly grasping.

"Yes. Thank you."

"I love this style. I'm so glad we have them in your size. I bet you look as cute as a button with them on."

Sicily glanced up and forced herself to smile. "They are great. It will be cash, please."

"Of course." The woman tilted her head as if studying Sicily. The dainty older woman pursed her lips as if trying to hold something behind them before ringing her up and sending her on her way.

Have them in my size? Did she mean to imply that the tent makers don't usually do this pattern?

Kari looked up as Sicily approached, a concerned smile on her pretty face. She had gotten her hair cut a month back and still looked impossibly beautiful with the style. It pulled in at her narrow face, framing her and helping to accentuate her button nose and brown eyes. Her blue blouse fit her snuggly, but it was a good look for her, Kari having been a runner her whole life. Dating the junior high coach in town was quite perfect for her and the two of them were beyond good for each other.

"You get the pants?"

"Yep." Sicily nodded toward the door. "I've had enough torture for the day. Let's go get a coffee and sit outside and enjoy this weather for a while."

"I'm completely down for that." Kari reached out and pressed the door open. "Lisa should be back in town tomorrow, right?"

"Yeah. I'm not sure how she and Marc are affording flying back and forth between Maine and New York every other weekend. When is he graduating?" Sicily reached up and pushed her hair behind her shoulder as the cool air of fall picked up around them.

Crimson, burnt orange and yellow leaves fluttered around their feet, the trees a sight to see that time of year. The fall season was the whole reason for Lisa and Sicily picking Maine as their locale for setting up shop and trying to start a new life. She glanced over at Kari, grateful for the girl being with them as well. Kari hadn't been part of the original plan for moving to Maine simply because she was engaged to be married to a guy who was born, and would die, in New York. Frank was a scoundrel and had cheated on Kari the night before the wedding.

Sicily reached out and took her friend's hand, squeezing it and smiling at her as Kari glanced over.

"Did you hear me? You look lost in thought." Kari squeezed back.

"Hm? Oh, I am. Did you tell me when Marc was graduating?"

"Yeah. It's next May from what momma told me. I swear Marc and I haven't spoken in a while. Just both so busy I guess."

"I need to call my brother, Johnny. It's been a few months since I've heard his voice too. That's just unacceptable. Life can be taken from you at any moment. Best to tell those you love how much they mean to you every chance you get. Right?" Sicily released Kari's hand as they walked into the quaint coffee shop.

Kari glanced over as sadness swept across her pretty features. Sicily's friends were empathetic to her situation with her mother, which helped, and yet didn't. She needed closure, but wasn't quite sure how to get it.

"The pumpkin spice coffee is finally back in season. I swear I want to get ten of them just to make up for the rest of the year when they don't have it." Kari smirked and moved toward the counter, glancing over her shoulder. "My treat."

"No. You paid last time." Sicily moved up beside her, handing her card to the handsome, young barista. "I'll pay for both of us."

"Of course, ma'am. What can I get you?" He glanced at Kari and then back to Sicily, his gaze almost analyzing.

He's disgusted by how fat you are. Hurry and order. Order something non-fat. Order it skinny or with no milk at all. Just get an espresso. No, you don't need anything. Get a water.

She swallowed the hot burn of disgust mixed with extreme sadness. Kari rolled her eyes at her before ordering, her friend not happy with not getting to pay.

"I'll have a medium pumpkin spice coffee with extra pumpkin spice and double the whipped cream."

"Now we're talking." The guy smiled at Kari and glanced to Sicily. "You want the same?"

He expects you to because you're the fat girl. Of course you want extra and doubles of everything.

"Uh, no. I'll take a glass of water, please." Sicily extended the card to him, the frown appearing on his face a replica to Kari's.

"No, she doesn't. She wants one of what I got." Kari reached out and tugged the card back.

"No. I don't." Sicily glanced toward her friend, a warning on her face. She was rarely terse with anyone, least of all Kari. They had been friends for the last two years and Kari was unbelievably loyal and kind. Sicily would rather slap a baby than hurt Kari's feelings.

"Sis... we've been waiting all year for these to come back. What's the deal?" Kari tilted her head, confusion on her face.

Sicily couldn't get into her issues in front of the handsome boy who seemed to be staring them down, waiting for some awkward cat fight that just wasn't going to happen.

"She's right." Sicily turned back to the guy. "I just had a big breakfast. Can you just make me a normal one with low-fat milk and no whipped cream please?"

"You bet. It's better the other way, but I'm happy to..."

Sicily cut him off, barking at him, which was far out of character for her. She felt like shit the minute she did it. "Low-fat milk. No whipped cream."

"Absolutely. It will be ready in a few minutes, girls." He smiled and nodded toward the pickup counter after checking them out.

Kari reached out and brushed her fingers down Sicily's arm and they moved to the counter. "Hey. What's going on? Talk to me."

Sicily glanced up and sucked her bottom lip into her mouth, pressing her teeth into it as tears filled her eyes again. She needed to get a hold of herself, but her damn weight was ruining her life, changing her personality, wrecking her sense of self-worth.

After all these years of being careful and taking care to keep herself healthy, she watched her mother die from heart disease and then decides to follow her?

A tear rolled down her face and she glanced toward the door. "Grab our drinks and I'll meet you outside."

She turned and walked out of the coffee shop, leaving Kari with most likely more questions than Sicily felt up to answering.

She just wanted to be left alone.

CHAPTER TWO

Sicily had done her best to push the conversation off the night before, Kari less than thrilled with her unwillingness to open up. How would she start a conversation like that anyway?

"I hate myself most days because I've gotten fat like my mother? I don't want anyone looking at me because all I see is condemnation and pity?"

Making a sharp left turn, she let out a soft growl and pulled up to the shop. A little red truck was parked in the spot beside hers, the young guy she hired at the end of the summer a god-send. Martin was nineteen and had just graduated in May from Bar Harbor High, but he wasn't yet sure what he wanted to do with his life, so his parents gave him a year to figure it out. He would be forced to go to college the following year. She was happy to have him as long as he could stay.

Sicily let her emotions wash out as she sat in the serenity of her car and forced herself to focus on the day she had ahead of her. The small square in the middle of the town had two bakeries and she was the one with all the sweets and treats. Judy's was more savory treats, but they had the occasional donut or muffin. The woman who owned it was a vicious bitch that Sicily tried to avoid like the plague.

She was too tall and thin for her own good. Her reasons behind owning the shop more to do with her insatiable desire to own the world than wanting to provide something delicious for the residents to enjoy. The plan from the on-start was to work the bitch out of business, but her elderly mother was actually the chef behind the efforts and after meeting her... Sicily couldn't do anything but help support the older woman when possible.

A smile lifted her lip as she thought about Lisa and Kari spending hours in the kitchen trying to decide what the three of them could do to put Judy's out of business. Two bakeries in a small town would never work, but somehow... it did.

She got out of the car and pulled her purse over her shoulder. Turning to glance around the square, she noticed a few cars outside the hardware shop, one of them seeming all too familiar.

Drake DeMarco.

Sicily rolled her eyes and walked quickly to the shop, wondering if she should park her car behind the store so that he wouldn't realize she was there. If he didn't stop by it would be a glorious day. The man had an incessant need to be in her face, offering her every deal he could come up with to join his gym. He seemed to like fixer-uppers and she wasn't interested in being one of his projects.

Being his for a long night of hot sex - anytime... unless she had to take off her clothes or he wanted to keep the lights on. She shook her head, realizing how ridiculous she was being. Drake wasn't interested in a relationship or sex. He wanted to help her lose weight and get healthy because that's how he made his money. Too bad he was Kari's boyfriend Jake's best friend. That simply meant he was in her life to stay. Good thing she had gotten quite comfortable with telling him to take a hike.

The problem was... he never did.

Martin pulled the door open with a big smile on his face. His shaggy blond hair was pulled back in a tight ponytail and his blue eyes filled with wonder.

Oh, to be young and hopeful again.

"Hey, boss lady. I was starting to wonder if you were coming in. You take one day off and all of a sudden you're late and I don't see the chocolate powder I texted you that we need." He moved back as Sicily walked in and reached out to brush a leaf off of her arm.

"Oh damn! You did ask me to pick that up." She turned as the door behind her opened.

Drake.

"Pick what up? Need me to go grab something for you guys? I don't have to be at the gym for a while." He slid his hand over his stomach, his movements accentuating the eight pack that lay beneath the tight t-shirt. The man had to be the most beautiful thing in all of Maine. His dark hair begged for someone's fingers to run through it over and over again. His eyes were almost black, his skin beautifully tanned and his personality that of an alpha male with world dominance in mind.

"No. We're good." Sicily turned back to Martin. "Do you need the powder this morning? I can run back out after I double-check inventory."

"We have an order at eleven, so I need it pretty soon." Martin glanced toward Drake. "Mr. DeMarco. How are you, Sir?"

Sicily moved toward the counter, dropping her purse in the open cabinet beside the register as the two guys started to talk about their long summer and how much Martin could lift now thanks to Drake's help. She tried to appear busy, not wanting to seem eager to hear anything Drake had to say. It had been a long six months of trying to hide how much she wanted to be a part of his life. He was far beyond her league when she was thin a few months back, but now... impossible.

No need to embarrass herself with hoping for something that would end in extreme rejection. Her friends badgered her nonstop about Drake, both of them misunderstanding his constant nagging for a crush. He wasn't interested in anything but her membership to his gym and the ability to tout to everyone that he had worked the town baker into shape. He was a dick most days - balking at her cooking and leaving her to feel like a walking heart attack, which she most likely was.

"I keep trying to get your boss to come see me." Drake moved toward the counter, tapping it as Sicily looked up.

"Oh yeah?" Martin moved up beside him, the wonder on the boy's face something Sicily was used to seeing. He wanted to be a chef and to own his own place. He was taken with her simply for that reason alone. She enjoyed it... it meant she was doing something right in some part of her life.

"I don't have time." She glanced back down, pressing a few buttons on the register to bring it to life. "Besides, no one trusts a thin chef."

"There's always time to work on your health, Sis," Drake responded.

She jerked her head up, her glare too harsh seeing that Martin took a step back. "I'm not interested in you soliciting in my shop today, Drake. It's Sicily and I'm busy. So is Martin."

"Sure am. Nice to see you again, Mr. DeMarco." Martin waved and slipped behind the counter, walking into the back room as Sicily held Drake's stare.

The determination on his handsome face was insanely hot. It took everything inside of her to push back the desire to agree to the training just to feel his hands on her, to spend more time with the cocky bastard.

"When are you going to stop pushing so hard against me?" He leaned in as she took a step back. No way was she ready for him intimidating her into their awkward partnership with him as trainer and her as the love-sick fat girl.

"When you back off. I'm not interested in having you put me with all the other trophies on your wall. I have work to do. By a full-fat pastry or get out." She crossed her arms over her chest.

A smirk lifted the side of his mouth and he nodded. "I'm going to get your chocolate powder. I'll be back shortly. You're coming to the gym tonight, not for me or anyone else, but for you."

"Are you calling me fat?" She lifted her eyebrow, her chest constricting painfully. She would not break down in front of him, or anyone other than her closest friends. If he attacked her in this moment she might not have a chance to push back her sorrow any further though.

"I would never do that. I'm sick of watching you mentally fuck yourself." He moved around the counter and she took another step back. "Stop running from me. I want to help you find yourself, Sicily. I'm not the dick you make me out to be."

"No clue what you're talking about." She shrugged and bent over, pulling a five dollar bill from her wallet. "Thanks for going on the errand for us."

He snatched the bill from her and growled softly. The sound of it rushed across her skin, searing its way down to the pit of her stomach and making her feel desire like she never had before.

Let it go. He's not interested in broken down chunky girls. He wants someone who takes care of themselves. That's certainly not you.

"Be at the gym at seven tonight. If you're not... I'm going to come and get you myself."

"Hogtie the hog?" She steeled her features, forcing herself to look hateful.

He started to respond before shaking his head and letting out a short, angry breath. Turning on his heel he walked out, letting the door slam.

She couldn't help but regret her last words. Now he would start thinking of her like the pig she was. She let out a long breath as the door to the kitchen opened and Martin stuck his head out.

"Coast clear? You okay?"

She nodded, swallowing her emotions. "Yeah. I'm good. You take the counter today. I want to bake. When Drake comes back just get the receipt and tell him I'm busy. I don't want to see him again." She walked toward the kitchen as Martin moved back for her.

"Why are you and Mr. DeMarco so tense with each other? Were you dating before?" Martin's voice was soft, caring.

"No. He wants a fixer-up and I'm not interested." She shrugged and started towards the back, Martin's response following her.

"He's after the wrong girl then."

The rest of the morning was busy filling various orders, but as always, things slowed down around two in the afternoon. Sicily finished cleaning everything up and stopped by the front to make sure Martin was done with his chores as well.

"Great day. We had tons of people in here. We might need to look at picking up holiday help if it keeps being so crazy." He smiled and leaned against the counter.

Peace sat on her for the first time in a long time, her cooking a large part of who she was and yet she had pushed the responsibility off to her only employee because he loved it too. She would have to split up their time in the kitchen to make sure they both got to do something they enjoyed and the shop still ran the way it was supposed to.

"That's not a bad idea. Let's put a sign on the door for part-time help. You think, like, ten to two Thursday through Sunday?"

"Absolutely. I'll see if I know anyone who might want to come help us." Martin pulled his keys from his pocket. "I'm headed to get a burger. Come with me?"

"I can't. I need to get home and help Kari with a few things. Next time." She winked at the kid, grateful for his kindness. He didn't seem to judge her, but simply accepted her for who she was.

"Rain check." He smiled and walked to the door. "See you tomorrow, boss."

"I'll be here." Sicily walked toward the door and locked it behind him. She watched him go and let out a long breath. She needed to try to start getting back in shape - on her own.

She kept a pair of shorts and an old t-shirt in her locker in the back, just on the off chance that she decided to actually do something about her lack of exercise. She made the decision to lock up and go for a short jog, allowing herself to walk when she needed to. Doing something was better than nothing.

Changing quickly before she could change her mind, she slipped out of the shop and locked it up. A chill picked up and ran across her, the air seeming to have dropped fifteen degrees. She let out a soft yelp and walked back into the shop, shivering.

"That's not happening."

She needed an indoor track or a treadmill. Picking up her purse, she left the shop, knowing that this would be a watershed moment in her journey to get healthy. She needed help, and though she hated herself for admitting it... Drake was the only one in town capable of helping her get her life back.

She would set up rules and lay down the law on him. As long as he stuck to them... she would come back the next day. For today she would just ask for the tour and the chance to run on one of his treadmills. Surely he would allow her that without plaguing her to death.

CHAPTER THREE

It took damn near forever to force herself out of the car when she got to the gym. The large brick building in front of her seeming far too commercialized for their sleepy town. The parking lot was half-full, which was surprising seeing that it was only three in the afternoon. Did all of the retired folks work out? Probably. Most of the people she had seen walking the streets were relatively healthy.

I'm in the minority here.

The door to the gym opened and Drake moved out, holding the door for an elderly couple. The smile on his face was kind, the expression reaching all the way to his eyes.

Sicily let out a long sigh, her heart fluttering in her chest. There was no way he would ever see anything but a project in her, but God if she didn't want him to.

He glanced toward her, a smile spreading across his mouth.

She couldn't help but stiffen as he walked toward her, waving once more to the older couple before stopping outside of her door.

Opening it, she stood up and looked him in the face. "I wanted to go for a jog, but it's too damn cold. Can I rent an hour on one of your treadmills?"

He chuckled, his eyes moving across her - judging her no doubt. "It doesn't work like that, but if you'll let me give you a tour of the place I might make an exception seeing that we're friends."

She moved out of the open door and closed it, trying like hell to appear calm and casual. "Is that what we are? Friends?"

"I'd come a'running if you called. I *think* that's what friends do."

She shrugged and walked toward the large building, the lights and sounds causing her heart to race slightly. The last time she had been in a gym was when she was a freshman in college, one of her boyfriends being quite taken with her, but asking her to lose a few pounds. He was concerned that she was gaining weight and he wasn't willing to date someone that didn't care for their body properly.

She'd joined the gym and he had slept with one of the trainers a week later. Great experience.

"So give me this tour and do your best to remind me that I'm overweight and need a membership. After I suffer through all of that trauma... I'd love to simply run in peace for about thirty minutes." She walked in and glanced over her shoulder, pinning him with a hard stare.

His athletic shorts were perfectly made for him, the large bulge at the front of them causing the air to rush from her lungs. She jerked her head around as heat burned her neck and chest. Surely he hadn't seen her ogling him.

How mortifying.

Drake moved up beside her and tapped his hand on the front desk as a pretty dark-haired girl walked up, her eyes brilliantly green. "Hey Drake. What's up?"

"This is Sicily Moretti. She's a friend of mine. Can you grab Violet and ask her to give Sicily a tour of the facilities?" He smiled kindly at the girl.

"Of course." She glanced toward Sicily. "Nice to meet you. I'm Jasmine. We'll have you fill out this liability form and then Violet will walk you around. She's uber nice."

"Oh." Sicily glanced at Drake, who winked and walked off. She couldn't help but follow him, the perfect swell of his rear leaving her wanting to let down her guard far more than she ever would. What the hell was wrong with her? Lisa was the sex addict. Sicily was much more like Kari. She wanted a solid friendship that moved into a relationship, and sex was a maybe after a lot of dates.

Drake was just the perfect body type for her wildest fantasies. That's one of the many reasons why she needed to stop fantasizing about him. He had taken center stage for far too many of her thoughts as of late. She found herself being more and more hostile toward him simply to protect herself.

"He's a great guy. You're a lucky girl if he calls you a friend." Jasmine smiled and picked up the phone, calling for Violet.

Sicily nodded, feeling like shit all of a sudden for expecting the worst from him. Maybe his pleas to get her into the gym weren't about scoring a buck, but simply because they belonged to the same close group of friends. She wanted it to be because he saw something romantically that he wanted to explore, but there was no way. He was far too much man for her.

"Hi there. I'm Violet. You must be Sicily?" A perky redhead stopped in front of her, extending her hand.

Sicily shook it and smiled. "Nice to meet you."

"You as well. Come on and I'll give you the grand tour." She nodded toward the free weight area, talking a little about it before moving to the large Olympic-sized pool. "You're friends with the big guy?"

"Um, yeah. Well, we're in the same friend group, so my best friend is dating his best friend." Sicily shrugged and pressed her hand against the warm glass where the pool was enclosed. "What are the hours on the pool?"

"Anytime we're open. You like to swim? It's great exercise."

"I do actually. I promised myself I wouldn't join this gym today, so know that I'm not signing anything." Sicily brushed her hand through her hair. "Not trying to be rude, but Drake's been after me for so long that I'm against giving in at this point."

She laughed and walked toward a hall of racquetball courts. "I totally understand. Just take the information with you and when you're ready, come see me and we'll get you started on a good program."

"I actually like racquetball. I played a little in college, though I'm not all that good."

"Practice makes perfect. It's all part of the package." Violet opened the door at the end of the hall and moved back. "This is the women's locker room. Let's show you the showers, lockers and sauna, and then we'll go to the cardio machines."

"Great. How long have you worked here?"

"Since Drake opened the place. He got here about six years ago when he was in his early twenties. Long story for his background, but I'm sure you know most of it."

"Yeah. I just wasn't sure if you were here from the beginning."

"Oh, yeah. I couldn't work for anyone else. He's like the brother I never had. Always taking care of all of us and giving back so much to the community. He helps the fire department when they run short. I guess his good friend is one of the guys up there."

"Yeah, Jake is my best friend's boyfriend, like I mentioned."

"Oh, cool. I didn't realize the connection."

They wrapped up the tour in front of the cardio machines, Violet extending her hand and smiling brightly.

"Glad to meet you, Sicily. Enjoy your complimentary workout and if you have questions or want more information, don't hesitate to call us. We'd be thrilled to have you join, but only when you're ready."

"Thanks. I appreciate your time."

Sicily waited until the pretty bombshell walked off before slipping in her ear buds and climbing up on the machine. She didn't want to look like a wuss, but flying off the back of the machine was out too. Drake might just want to be friends, but she still felt the need to look as bad-ass as she was capable of pulling off in front of him.

She cranked it up and jumped onto the moving belt, her music pumping in her ears and her heart picking up speed. The first few minutes felt good, her blood pumping and energy rushing through her system. After the first lap around the electronic track, a hitch started to throb in her side and she was forced to slow down, walking quickly, and then limping until she had to stop the machine.

Pressing her palm to her head, she leaned over and tried to catch her breath, not caring at all who was watching. Dying in front of everyone was out, but she might not have a choice. She jerked up as a hand touched her back.

"Sicily. You okay?" Drake's concern was evident in his voice and all over his face.

Probably worried about your fat ass keeling over and him getting sued.

"Hmm?" She was having trouble making out all of the words he spoke. The blood was pumping in her ears far too fast. Holding on tightly to the machine, she leaned forward, needing to rest her head against her arms again.

"Here. Let me get you off of this. You can't go from zero to two hundred percent on day one, pretty girl." Drake's arms were around her, lifting her up and carrying her to a nearby chair.

She kept her eyes adverted, in hopes of not witnessing the stares of everyone around her who was in enough shape to jog on a machine without keeling over. Horror rolled over her.

Drake had probably almost pulled his back out having picked her up. She glanced up at him as he squatted in front of her. If he was hurt, he held it in well.

There was no hiding her weight after he picked her up. He would be more than aware of her obesity.

"Hey. It's okay. Tell me that you're all right." He reached up and touched the side of her face, his thumb wiping away a tear that dripped out of the side of her eye. She hadn't realized she was crying.

"How embarrassing," she whispered and sat back, forcing herself to smile as another round of tears rolled down her face.

Drake reached around her and handed her a soft white hand towel. "Nothing to be embarrassed about. Everyone comes in here ready to kick ass. That's why I don't usually let them work out for a few weeks without one of us. Your mind is willing, but we need to wake your body up. You and everyone else have to go through this."

She nodded, unsure of what to say. She needed to change the subject, and fast. A loud crack resounded, saving her from having to say anything. Drake stood up and turned around, his shoulders flexing as he growled.

"Stay here and rest. I'll be back."

Sicily sunk down into her chair and pulled the towel down her face as Drake's voice rose full of authority and dominance.

"I told you not to drop those weights again. It scares everyone in here. Get your stuff and we'll talk later. You're not welcomed in here anymore today."

The large man he spoke to was easily his height, but a bit larger. The guy laughed and shook his head.

"Fuck you, dude. I pay my membership. You can take a ticket and get in line with all the other bitches to give me hell over something stupid." The guy picked up another barbell.

Drake walked around him and tugged the barbell out of his hands before putting it down and lifting up in front of him. "I'm not going to tell you again to get packing."

"Whatcha gonna do? You're just a pretty boy with a big mouth and a few dollars in your pocket."

Sicily let out a yelp as the guy swung at Drake. The gym owner moved with far more flexibility than Sicily thought possible. He had the guy on the floor on his chest with his hands behind his back. Drake pressed his knee firmly into the guy's back.

"Vi, call the cops and have them come pick up old Cliff. He can't seem to respect the rules."

"Will do boss." Violet moved fast, her hands shaking, as if she expected something worse to have happened.

Where did Drake get his skills from? Gyms didn't teach self-defense. Was he a cop or in the military before coming to Bar Harbor?

After waiting a few minutes, she finally felt as if the world had stopped moving. Standing up carefully, she walked toward the front door and slipped out. Drake was busy with the cops and the big guy who seemed to be well-known for his temper.

Some part of her wanted to wait until they could talk, but she wasn't sure what she would say anyway. Sorry for being a fatty and crumbling on the treadmill? Just didn't seem as sexy as she wanted to be. Maybe he could be her incentive to get in shape and look better. Maybe he would consider something more than a friendship with her in the future.

No. She would lose weight in hopes of that, have him reject her, and then she would start the cycle all over again. She had to do this for herself if she had any hope of making it stick.

CHAPTER FOUR

The last thing she wanted was to have a dinner date with Lisa and Kari, but there was no getting out of it. They had pushed her toward the shower, both of them cheering because of her going to the gym. She had agreed to go out to dinner if they chose someplace with a healthy menu and promised to shut up about Drake.

What was it with the two of them? Drake wasn't interested in her and yet they both nagged non-stop about him. They were nagging the wrong half of the equation. She resigned herself to putting on a fake smile and making it through the evening. She would analyze her epic fail on the treadmill later over a shot of tequila and a good cry. Having Drake be the one to carry her off the machine had sealed the deal.

She wasn't joining his gym - ever.

"Come on already. I'm fucking starving out here." Lisa's voice came through the bathroom door as Sicily worked to get her brush through her wet, tangled mess of hair.

"I'm coming. Get a snack. I just went shopping on Wednesday." She worked faster, hating to be the reason why her friends were waiting.

A long sigh followed by another bang on the door. "Okay. Just hurry. I want to catch up."

"You were gone for three days." Sicily laughed unable to help herself. Lisa was the toughest and least needy out of all of them, but something about dating Marc, Kari's brother, had changed the feisty redhead. To some degree it was for the better. They almost seemed to soften the rough edges of one another.

"I know. I'm turning into a total puss," Lisa groaned.

"Vulgar. Jeez." Sicily turned to the mirror and smiled. She and Lisa had been friends since elementary school, their lives intertwined around each other's for as long as she could remember. Through thick and thin they had been there for each other and moving to Maine together just seemed a great end to the story.

"It's not the end. It's the beginning," Sicily mumbled under her breath and leaned in to apply her eye make-up. She might have gained a few pounds, but there was no way in hell she wasn't going to put the effort forward to look good for girl's night out. She might just meet the man of her dreams. She had to look the part in case fate was turning a blind eye and cutting her some slack for the evening.

Working quickly, she towel dried her hair and wrapped the small terrycloth around herself before slipping out of the bathroom and moving to her bedroom. Lisa whistled behind her and Sicily shook her head.

Lisa had no couth and no sense of modesty, nor had she ever. Sicily started to close her bedroom door only to feel the tension of Lisa pushing it open.

"Let me in." Lisa slipped in and closed the door before flopping down on Sicily's bed.

"I'm changing. Give me two minutes."

"No. I've seen you naked a thousand times. Get dressed and let's go." Lisa rolled onto her back and extended her hands into the air, her nails natural and long. "It was good to see Marc, but I'm ready for him to come here. I missed you guys."

"I missed you too." Sicily started to kick her best friend from the room and decided against it. Lisa *had* seen her a million times over the years strutting her stuff, but never before had she been so overweight.

"What's up with you? You seem uncomfortable. I can leave if it's going to fuck with you this bad."

Sicily turned to face Lisa, a grimace replacing the calm demeanor she was going for. "It's not that. I'm just so damn fat right now."

"You are not." Lisa sat up and lifted an eyebrow. "You've gained a few pounds, but in all the right places. Your boobs are bigger, your ass more round."

"Whatever. My thighs touch and my stomach has more rolls than my bakery." Sicily shrugged and dropped the towel, walking to her dresser and slipping into a pair of big white panties that made her feel small.

"That's stupid and those panties aren't happening." Lisa got up and walked up to the dresser, pulling out a small black G-string that was sure to get lost somewhere in her ass during the night. "Here. Wear these."

"No. Not happening." Sicily took them and dropped them back in the drawer. "I'm so unbelievably out of shape right now. Kari had to take me to get new pants, which were two sizes bigger than the ones I wore earlier this year."

"Earlier this year your mother died and you went through a massive depression, Sis. You look so much better now. Your body is curvy and fucking hot." Lisa glanced down at her, reaching out to brush her hand over Sicily's back. "Stop fooling yourself. Drake DeMarco isn't the type of man to go for someone less than smoking hot."

"He's not going for me." Sicily tossed the panties back in the drawer and walked to the closet, pulling a bra from one of the hangers and tugging down a formless black winter dress.

"Yes, he is. I've seen the way he looks at you." Lisa moved up beside her again, picking up a large brown belt and boots. "Wear this with your dress. It will accentuate your waist."

"I don't want anything accentuated. I want to hide in a big hole and starve myself until I drop twenty pounds." Sicily took the boots and belt, knowing it was far easier just to dress up than argue with Lisa.

"You're overreacting. You always have about your weight." Lisa moved toward the bed and took Sicily's shoulders, turning her. "You're not your mother. You are beautiful and the perfect size for a handsome man like Drake to wrap himself around. He's interested in so much more than your body and your beauty though. It's your willingness to open the shop, your intellect and your humor... honestly, just you. You're perfectly well-rounded."

"I know. I need to watch what I get tonight. My roundness is the problem." Sicily pulled from her friend and started to get dressed. "I'll be out in a minute. I'm done talking about this. It's depressing."

Lisa started up again and Sicily turned to her, putting a hand on her hip and making sure her old friend was well aware that she was done with the topic at hand.

Lisa lifted her hands and let out a snort. "Fine. You're being unreasonable, but I'll let you come to the conclusion on your own. You're beautiful. Period. End of conversation."

Sicily started to reply, but Lisa had already walked out of the room.

Good. She was simply trying to make me feel better. That's what friends do.

"So how is it having Martin Wilcox work for you?" Lisa asked as she leaned up between the front seats as they drove back home from dinner.

"It's good. He's a great kid." Sicily glanced back at her friend as Kari sang to the song on the radio and drove.

Dinner was filling and Sicily had worked hard to keep it light. Her friends ate their usual fare of fattening meats slathered in butter and cheese with pasta and tons of bread. It took all of the willpower she could find not to dive into the sinful meal with them. The image of Drake scowling down at her at the gym caused her to keep her hands in her lap.

Had he scowled? No.

Why did she replace his kindness with him basically attacking her for not being able to run on the machine? Protection.

She was beginning to want more than a casual bantering friendship with him and where she was a strong girl, her heart couldn't handle rejection right now.

"Are the guys coming over tonight?" Lisa asked, moving back, but catching Sicily's attention.

"What guys? Is Marc in town already? You just got back." Sicily tugged at her seatbelt, her heart working to beat its way out of her chest at the thought of seeing Drake.

"Drake and Jake are coming over for dessert." Kari glanced over, smiling like the villain she was.

"What? Why?" Sicily let out a long sigh. "I don't have anything made. Stop by the bakery and I'll get a cake from the counter cabinets. I think there were some small chocolate ones left."

"No. They're bringing something." Kari turned the radio down.

"Knowing Drake it's probably fruit." Lisa chuckled and patted Sicily's shoulder. "Don't get all worked up. He likes you way more than you like him."

"That's good because I don't like him at all." She jerked her head around, her voice giving her emotions away no doubt.

All she got was several "um hm's". She leaned back in her seat and closed her eyes as nausea rolled through her. She wasn't ready to face Drake after the events of earlier, but as usual - what choice did she have?

They were at the house within minutes, both Jake and Drake's trucks sitting out front. Sicily let out a quiet groan and got out of the car, wishing like hell she was wearing something a little less revealing. The dress clung to her, the belt making it hard to breathe and most likely cutting her in half.

Lisa and Kari were to the door before she made it past the gravel drive, the chill of late fall causing her to shiver. She would have preferred to split off from the group and just stand by herself on the back porch, but that wasn't going to happen. At least not yet.

Kari opened the door and walked in as Lisa looked over her shoulder, extending her hand and smiling.

"You and I are going to have a long talk soon. This girl you're becoming isn't the one I grew up with. I don't like it."

"I don't either. I'm just not sure how to change it." Sicily reached for her friend and forced a smile before slipping into the house.

Kari was wrapped in a tight hug with Jake, the sound of their kissing causing Sicily to turn away. She didn't want to interrupt their private moment, though they were rarely private. Drake was in the kitchen, his back to her. The jeans he wore sat low on his hips, his rear still doing a beautiful job of filling them up.

She moved into the kitchen as he glanced over his shoulder, his dark eyes moving across her body and stopping on her face.

"Don't you look stunning?" His tongue snaked out as he licked at his fingers, red juice dripping from the thick digits.

Sicily adverted her eyes and moved toward the sink, muttering 'thanks' before washing her hands. He was being kind. After the drama of earlier, he seemed to feel the need to make her feel better. Maybe he wasn't the cock she made him out to be. The girls at the gym seemed to adore him in a brotherly sense. Had he dated any of them?

Sicily glanced over her shoulder as Jake and Lisa started teasing each other. She couldn't hear exactly what their bantering was about, but caught Drake's gaze again. He leaned against the counter and watched her intently. His predatory stare moved across her again, his tongue licking at his full lips.

She shivered and turned back to the sink as the air seemed so hard to breathe. Was she making things up or had he just eye-fucked her? It took a few minutes to get her nerves to calm down, Lisa helping the situation by coming in and joining them.

"What are we doing over here?" She wrapped an arm around Sicily.

"Washing my hands. I was going to help with the strawberries that Drake was cutting up."

Drake moved up on her left and slid his arm around her lower back, Sicily stiffening at his touch.

"No need, pretty girl. I already got them done. If you have whipped cream we could just top the dessert off. I would have brought vanilla cake, but my favorite bakery is closed." He winked as she glanced over at him.

"It's going to be closed more often too if I don't get some help." She shook both of them off carefully, moving from the sink and picking up a hand towel.

"Are you hiring for the fall?" Lisa asked, moving to the table and plopping down.

"Just for the holidays. It's so busy, we can't keep up with orders and manning the store at the same time." She shrugged.

"It can't be that hard. Just adjust your hours. You're hardly ever there." Drake crossed his arms over his chest, his words harsh, but expression kind and caring. He was forever a contradiction.

"I'll keep that in mind. Thanks for the advice." She rolled her eyes and dropped the towel. "I'm going for some air. I'll be back in a minute."

She walked down the hall and slipped out onto the porch. Letting out a long breath, she moved to rest her arms against the railing, hoping like hell everyone would leave her alone.

The door opened behind her and she ignored it. Probably Lisa checking on her.

Drake moved beside her, placing his arms on the railing too and nudging her with his shoulder. "I wanted to check on you from earlier. You doing okay?"

"Yeah. Just overdid it. I used to run every day, but it's been a while." She shrugged.

"Are you working out now for your health or to lose weight?"

She glanced toward him as anger rose in her belly. "Are you saying I need to lose weight?"

He turned and took her by the shoulders, turning her toward him. "Why are you so incredibly defensive with me? I asked you a simple question. I implied nothing."

"You did too and you have several times. I've gained weight since getting here. I know. I'm working on getting rid of it. Stop asking me to join your damn gym. I'm not a project or a..." She didn't get the last bit out.

He pulled her close and slipped his arms around her, holding her tightly as he pressed his lips to hers. Sicily fought against him for a moment before sinking into his hold. He smelled far too good, his strength weakening her and his lips so far beyond soft.

She moved back as his tongue brushed across her lips, soft pants leaving her. "Too much. Too soon."

"No. I've been waiting too long to do that." He held on tightly. "What are you afraid of?"

"You judging me. You don't know the half of it."

"I could say the same." He ran his hands over her back. "You're not a project to me. I see your desire to gain your health back and I want to help. Stop making me into a villain. I'm not. I'm a friend."

"I'll try." She glanced down, wanting to snuggle deep into his hold and press her lips to the muscle running up the side of his sexy throat. "Let me go."

"Join my gym and let me help you do whatever it is that you're trying to do."

"Fine, but I have rules." She pulled out of his hold and took a long breath.

He was too much. The needy way he watched her, the aggressive way he took ahold of her, the deep, commanding sound of his voice. She could melt into a puddle at his feet, and just might, if she didn't get back inside and keep herself protected from him.

"Tell me the rules and I'll follow them as best I can. I'm a bad boy by nature, just so you know."

"Somehow I knew that." She smirked, unable to help herself. "Don't touch me again. Don't demand anything of me. And don't hover over the top of me at the gym."

He nodded and she turned to walk back into the house, her body aching with need for the sexy bastard behind her that would take her heart and destroy it. Why were all of her rules desperately needed in the context of the bedroom where she wouldn't get them and not in the gym where she would?

CHAPTER FIVE

Sicily had simply excused herself the night before, Lisa checking on her once as she lay in the darkness of her bedroom. She couldn't face Drake again, knowing that he either wanted something more with her, or was playing a dangerous game. She would root out the truth, but until she had the strength to push him back she needed to try and keep the private time between the two of them to a minimum. She would join the gym, but ask for Violet to be her trainer if they felt she needed one.

Keeping things casual with Drake would be hard, but doable.

She dressed in a pair of jeans, a t-shirt, and tennis shoes. A navy blue cardigan helped to hide everything she didn't want anyone to see. Her breasts were bigger, but they simply aided in making her look more portly rather than more feminine.

She stopped by the bathroom to put her hair into a high ponytail and put on a little make-up. She was needed at the bakery that morning to work on a large wedding cake order they had for later that day. Most of the prep work was done the day before, but the icing needed to be fresh for the event.

Martin needed to sleep in, the poor kid looked like a zombie last Saturday morning when they opened early. She had given him a late start time and almost looked forward to the serenity that the empty shop would provide.

Walking into the kitchen, Sicily stopped short as Kari and Lisa spoke in hushed whispers.

"So how do we set them up?" Kari asked, leaning into her friend as they appeared to be looking out the window toward the porch and large lake that sat at the edge of the property.

"Talk to Jake. I don't know Drake, but he seems a little reserved too. Find out if he's into Sis or if he's just naturally a flirt."

"Okay, but don't say anything to her. She doesn't seem to like him at all."

"That's because she likes him too much. Mum's the word. Let's help our girl out."

Sicily moved back into the hall, clearing her throat as she rounded the corner.

"Hey guys. I'm headed to the shop." She walked to the coffee pot as they moved away from each other, the two looking far guiltier than they should.

"Oh, good. You want to have lunch?" Kari asked, pulling her phone out of her pocket. "Damn, never mind. I have a shooting for the paper at eleven. Dinner?"

"Sounds good. When is Marc coming into town, Lisa?" Sicily poured her a travel mug of coffee and stood over the cream and sugar, arguing with herself internally about whether to add it. The coffee tasted like shit without it, and yet drinking your calories had always been a no-no.

"Next week on Friday. I'm ready for him to come now."

"Miss him?" Sicily decided against the sugar, but added a small scoop of cream. She turned and stirred the caramel-colored liquid, waiting for Lisa to respond.

"Of course, but is it bad that I miss his dick more than him?"

"Vulgar." Sicily turned and walked to the door, calling her goodbyes behind her as Kari made gagging sounds and Lisa laughed loudly. She couldn't help but chuckle at her friends and their silliness.

There might be a lot of tragedy in her past and struggle in her current situations, but the warmth provided by having good friends that filled the house with laughter left tomorrow looking bright.

Sicily spent most of the early morning getting the wedding order complete. Standing back with a small camera, she took a few pictures and smiled, the vision before her beyond beautiful. She was grateful for her talent, but could use a break on the desire to cave in to her sweet tooth. It had been a few days since she had tasted any of the pastries, which was highly unusual. Watching her weight was an extreme challenge simply because of the environment that she was immersed in all the time.

The clock struck nine and she opened the door, spending the next few hours talking with customers, taking orders and selling a variety of goodies. By the time Martin showed up she was worn out.

"Hey, boss. You look pretty today. The blue brings out the brightness in your eyes." He smiled and pulled an apron from the hanger on the wall.

"Thanks. I'm going to disappear into the back. Call me out if someone needs me or you do."

"I always need you." He wagged his eyebrows. The kid was beyond cute.

"I could be your mother." She shook her head and walked to the back, his rebuttal following her.

"Six years, Sicily. It's only six years difference between us."

She let the door close behind her before pressing her hands to the cold slab in front of her. Her head dropped, chin to her chest as she closed her eyes. She wanted to find Drake, to force him to pull her close again. Why had he taken her in his arms and kissed her the night before? Didn't he know that she was fragile? That she needed affection so bad to find value in herself? It was no way to live, but she couldn't seem to move past it.

"Maybe it was pity?" she whispered into the empty room as tears stung her eyes. Wiping them away, she turned quickly as the door opened.

"Someone's here to see you, boss."

"I'll be right there." She kept her back to Martin, pretending to be on her phone. It was most likely someone from the wedding or Drake. He seemed to show up at the most inappropriate of times.

Taking a deep breath, she steeled her resolve to be mature and walked out to find a handsome older man waiting at the front counter for her.

"I'm Sicily. Did you ask for me?"

"Do you own this bakery?" The handsome gentleman extended his hand. His smile was nice, but something in his gaze told her that he was far more than he appeared.

"I do. What can I do for you?"

"I'm Michael Carrington. I was seeing your friend Lisa for a little while. I do believe she mentioned you multiple times."

"Oh." Sicily shook his hand and moved out from behind the counter, nodding to a small table in the corner. "We can talk over here if you like. I see another rush of kids headed this way."

Michael glanced behind him, his suit fitting him beautifully. "They do look rather rambunctious, but I have no room to talk. I still feel like I'm ten somewhere deep inside this aging body."

She chuckled and moved to the table, taking a seat and extending her hand to offer him the other one. He unbuttoned his coat and sat down as the door opened. Drake walked in and caught her gaze, heading her way as if Michael weren't even there.

He stopped short, glancing over at Michael as a smile lifted his lips. "Michael Carrington. It's been a while."

Michael stood back up and laughed loudly, extending his hand and pulling Drake into a hug. "Oh my goodness. It's been years. How is your family? Demetri still trying to rule the universe?"

"Only his small part of it. How is Cynthia?"

"Oh. She passed about five years back. Aggressive form of cancer." Michael glanced down as a frown darkened his handsome face.

"You guys know each other from way back?" Sicily couldn't help but ask.

Drake turned his attention to her. "Yeah. We used to be business partners back in our younger days. My brother introduced us."

"Great guy. Great family." Michael released his hold on Drake and sat down, leaning back and smiling.

"I'm sorry to hear about your wife. So good to see you." Drake glanced at Sicily. "I'm going to wait over there."

"For what?" She pressed her forearms against the table.

"To take you to lunch. I was just going to swing by, but I'm sure this scoundrel will try if I don't swoop in and save you." He winked at Michael.

"You know I can't resist a beautiful woman." He tilted his head, his smile almost nefarious.

Sicily's cheeks heated and she waved Drake off. "Stop, you damn flatterers. Lunch sounds good."

Drake chuckled and walked away, leaving her a hot mess with butterflies tearing up the inside of her stomach. She turned her attention to the handsome billionaire in front of her, trying to clear her mind.

"What can I do for you, Mr. Carrington?"

"There is a large benefit for the fire station coming up in November and I'd like to provide the dessert table. Would you be willing to work with me on catering it?"

"Of course. I can spare quite a bit in terms of donating items too. I don't mind."

"No. Not at all. I'm paying for every bit of it. You can simply make the items or you can make them and be there to assist me in running the event. I know you're a chef and obviously a smart business woman. I'd love your help. I'll pay generously for your time."

"How can a girl say no?"

"Oh, please do tell Drake that you can't say no to me." The handsome man before her laughed and lifted his eyebrow. "We used to be after the same woman in our younger years."

"Who got her?"

"I did, and I loved her until the day she died." He smiled sadly and reached for his wallet. "Draw up the order and let's get you paid and locked in as my cohort for the event."

She moved numbly to the back, glancing over at Drake, who seemed to be suffering the effects of Michael's news. What business were they involved in together? Was the town really that little? The world that small?

CHAPTER SIX

"Tell me how you know Mr. Carrington?" Sicily walked outside with Drake. She glanced around the parking lot looking for his truck, but didn't see it. "Am I driving?"

"No. I brought the bike. That okay?" He walked to a decked out Harley and pulled a spare helmet off the back, tossing it to her.

Sicily caught it as her words escaped her. She had spent a large part of her teenage years riding on the back of motorcycles, her older brother owning several as a mechanic. It had been years since she felt the thrill they provided. The fear that rushed through her was simply over being so close to Drake and nothing to do with the inherent danger of riding on the back of a bike.

"Yeah. It's fine," she muttered and slipped the helmet on before walking to get on behind him.

"Just hold on to me tightly and we'll be good. I'll tell you about me and Mike at the restaurant." He started the bike as she slid her hands around his waist.

The thick muscles of his abs tensed under her fingers. She had to bite her lip to stifle the moan that pressed against her tongue. He was so far beyond sexy and yet complete trouble.

One thing her brother, Johnny, had made her promise to do was never date a guy who had a bike. She smiled at the memory of asking him why.

"Any man that wants power between his legs usually replies in kind with his woman. You need someone gentle and caring to love you. Not some sex hungry bastard."

"You have bikes." She lifted her eyebrow at him and smirked.

"Exactly. Stay far away from those guys."

"Like you."

"Hush and get on the bike."

She laughed as Drake took off, his hand brushing by her fingers as if to tell her that he heard her joy and wanted more of it from her.

The ride to the edge of town was thrilling, Drake driving a bit too wild, but she loved every minute of it. Since going to college and trying to care for her mother through her illness, fun hadn't been too big a part of her life in a while. Being with Lisa and Kari was her only reprieve, but those times had just begun. A few months back there only seemed to be darkness in front of her - behind her... everywhere.

Drake stopped the bike and parked it before waiting for her to get off. He twisted his torso and extended his hand to her, Sicily taking it and getting off. She glanced around the harbor and stifled a squeal. She had been planning on coming down to the small shopping village and trying their clam chowder and getting lost for a day or so in the shops. With the new shop she just hadn't gotten the opportunity.

It was so not Lisa's type of place, but Kari would have joined her. She moved back and tugged the helmet off, Drake reaching over and helping her. She reached up and ran her fingers through her hair as he affixed the helmets to the back of the bike.

He slid his fingers through the back of her hair, his eyes narrowing only slightly. "I knew it."

"What?" She swatted him away.

"Your hair looks like dark silk. I've been wanting to test the theory since we met."

"Yes, well, keep your hands to yourself. We're friends, and barely that."

"As of now..." He wagged his eyebrows and pointed to the small bistro ahead. "Best clam chowder in this whole state. You wanna try it?"

"I do. I've wanted to since we came to visit a while back and decided this was going to be home."

"I'm glad you did." He winked at her and walked toward the small shop, his fingers grazing by hers several times. If she didn't know any better, he wanted to hold her hand. She was beyond grateful that he didn't push it - didn't push her. She wasn't ready mentally. Physically she was panting on the inside, desperate to feel every inch of him against her, inside of her, suffocating her.

All right. Enough. Shit.

They walked into the restaurant and seated themselves near a window, the colors of fall brilliant just outside the restaurant. Sicily pressed her hand to her chin and leaned toward it, wanting to take it all in. Where was Kari with her camera when you needed her?

"Beautiful." Drake's voice was soft and far too low.

Sicily glanced at him as her cheeks burned. "I know, right? I've been waiting for fall to arrive since we got here."

"The scene outside is okay, but the one in here is breathtaking." He picked up his menu and watched her for a minute before glancing down.

He played a dangerous game. One she couldn't afford to lose. After she lost her extra weight and got healthy she would flirt back and open herself up to going on a date with him, but not a second sooner. If he really did want something from her, then he deserved her healthy and completely able to sustain life. If not, then she would be better suited to handle that rejection once she felt better about herself.

The waiter approached them and they each ordered, Drake making her promise to save room for dessert.

"I thought you didn't eat anything unhealthy." She scoffed at him before pulling her napkin into her lap. They looked ridiculous together. Him tall, dark, muscular and devastatingly handsome and her just... fat and plain.

"I don't usually indulge unless I find something I just can't say no to." He held her stare, his words seeming to mean more than the simple dessert she was referring to.

"Then we'll have whatever you're wanting." She glanced down and picked up her water glass, taking a quick sip. "Tell me about Michael. If everyone thinks you're dead... he obviously doesn't now."

"He knows the set up. He helped with it a little. Him and my brother are close."

"He and Lisa dated a little earlier this year before she finally started seeing Marc."

"Did they really?" Drake chuckled. "Why am I not surprised by that? Lisa is very much his type of woman. Bold, flashy and addicted to sex."

"How do you know she's addicted to sex?"

"She's bold and flashy. Everyone knows." He smiled and the room seemed to brighten.

"What type of woman would you say is your type? If you and Michael cared for the same woman, then is bold and flashy your type too?" Sicily slipped her hands in her lap, pissed at herself for bringing it up. It was a cornered conversation that she prayed would result in her being his type, and yet she knew nothing could become of them.

"That type of woman used to be what I went after, but the world I lived in before this one was dark and filled with sadness and death. I needed bright and flashy to keep my mind off of everything around me." He leaned back and rubbed his chest a few times.

She started to ask why he did that. He seemed self-consumed, touching his chest and abs all the time, but maybe that wasn't it at all. His other comment had her, but he spoke up again before she could.

"Now, my type of woman would be someone who knows how to look past my scars and love me for the man I might become.

I'll never be great, but I'm working on being good." He shrugged, his answer tugging at her heart.

"And you knowing Michael. He said you were once in business together. Was that in your darker days, as you put it?"

"Yeah. I'll explain more when I can. I really don't want you running out on our first date. That would defeat all of this wise-ass tension we've been building up since you arrived in Bar Harbor." He smirked and glanced up to the waiter, who delivered them each a beer.

She waited until he left to ask her question. "Is this a date?"

"I hope it is. I want it to be."

"Why? I'm not at all the type of woman who fits next to you, Drake. We're friends. Nothing more."

"You're not interested? Not in the slightest?"

"I'm interested in knowing more about you, in learning how to be healthy from you, in growing a friendship, but anything else... no."

"I understand. I have more work to do, obviously." He chuckled, his resolve seeming to only grow where she was concerned.

She needed to move away from the conversation about them. "Tell me about your brother. Is he still in Chicago?"

"He sure is. My grandparents were immigrants from Italy in the thirties and my grandfather worked hard to build himself up as a businessman in Chicago. They opened loads of restaurants, but through a few too many hardships, they turned to a different string of businesses. My mom and dad had eleven of us. I'm in the middle somewhere. My older brother, D, is still there and my sister helps him with some of the businesses around. A few of my other siblings are involved, but I honestly needed a fresh start. I was always finding trouble and getting into the worst fucking situations ever. My brother asked me seven years ago after another long string of bad decisions if I wanted out. I said yes. There was a cost associated with getting me replanted somewhere else. I lost contact with most of them. They think I'm dead. Only Demetri knows the truth." He shrugged and picked up his beer, taking a long drink of it.

"Why would they need to think you're dead, Drake? What did you do?"

"I'm not ready to let you in that far just yet. You're the first woman I've wanted to take on a date in five years. Let me take baby steps and I'll give you the chance to judge me like everyone else has."

"I wouldn't do that." Sicily reached across the table, knowing all too well what it felt like to be judged.

He chuckled, the sound sad and falling flat in front of her. "You'd be the first if you didn't."

CHAPTER SEVEN

One Week Later

The rest of the week was filled with trying to keep the shop afloat and searching high and low for someone to help fill in. It just wasn't happening. For some reason everyone in Bar Harbor was employed or too old. Drake had appeared on her doorstep a few times, offering to take her to lunch or asking her to go for a walk. She refused out of necessity to get things done at the shop, but the few times they did get together it was in the comfort of their friends.

Sicily hated to watch the fire inside of him dwindle, but whatever he was fighting against, he seemed to be losing. She joined the gym during the week and asked for Violet to help train her, the girl sweet and immediately becoming a much needed force of positivity in Sicily's life.

The week had ended, and with Marc coming into town that night, everyone was excited. Being around Lisa, one couldn't help but take on some of the joy that overflowed in the air around the pretty redhead.

Sicily walked into the house Friday afternoon and let out a soft chuckle. Marc stood up from the table and moved toward her, picking her up in a bear hug. They had grown close as friends over the last six months, the guy too much like a brother not to let him into her heart.

"I swear you're paying more for this traveling back and forth with Lisa than you are on school." Sicily moved back and teased him playfully.

"No shit, right? My girl won't let me quit school, but each time we have to leave each other that option sounds more and more enticing." He glanced over his shoulder as Lisa walked up and popped his butt.

"We're going dancing tonight. We're grabbing a sandwich here and then we'll meet up with Kari, Jake and Drake at the club. Let's get rolling on dinner and then go get dressed, chica. Tonight's the night you get laid." Lisa reached out and tugged at a long strand of Sicily's hair.

"Um, no it's not." Sicily shook her head and moved around her friends into the small kitchen. Marc and Lisa had already laid out a spread of sandwich options. Her stomach growled angrily as she picked up a pickle and popped it into her mouth.

"What? Why not? Drake is totally into you. Sex would be a great release for you, Sis." Lisa moved up beside her and wrapped an arm around her neck.

"Firstly, I'm not discussing my pathetic sex life in front of Marc, nor am I in the mood to put on something tight and shake my fat ass."

"Your ass is actually super nice." Marc moved up beside Lisa, putting his arms around her neck.

Sicily snagged a piece of turkey and moved into the hall as Lisa agreed with her man.

"I'm not listening to this. I'm getting in my pajamas." Sicily walked into her room and noticed a card on her bed. She picked it up and opened it, the message from Drake.

Hey,

Not sure I can make it to the club tonight. I'm waiting to hear from my brother. My mom's not been doing too well. Just didn't want you to think I was standing you up.

Lunch soon. I want to see you. Stop putting me off. Friends - remember?

~D

Concern filled her chest as she reached for her phone, wanting to check on his mom. She stopped herself, realizing that she couldn't do anything to help him anyway. They weren't together, and any comfort she offered him would simply be out of her need to be something important to him.

Lisa showed up in the door of her room and knocked on the door frame. "Come with us. Please."

"No. I'm tired and this note from Drake says he's not going. How did it get here?"

"He stopped by a little while ago and asked me to give it to you. I didn't want to forget, so I dropped it on the bed." Lisa walked in and pulled Sicily into a hug. "You sure about tonight?"

"Yes. Don't force me. I'm tired and honestly can't imagine anything better than a long, hot bath and a night in front of the TV."

"Okay. I understand. Don't wait up for us. It's party animal time."

Marc let out a long howl from the kitchen, the man having ridiculously good hearing.

Sicily laughed and pointed to the door. "Close that on your way out."

Her phone buzzed as Lisa slipped out. It was Drake. Twice in one day was a little odd.

Drake: You there?

Sicily: Yeah. How are you? Mom doing okay?

Drake: Why does it feel good to hear you call her Mom?

Sicily: Don't be a girl. Your mom, not mine, silly. Are you okay?

> **Drake:** Forever withdrawn from me. Yeah, I'm good. She went into the hospital, but D says she's out. I need to go see her, but...

Sicily: She doesn't know you're alive?

Drake: No one does. So fucking lonely sometimes without all of them.

Sicily: I understand. I miss my family too. Especially my mom.

Drake: You guys close?

Sicily: I lost her in January. Heart attack from obesity.

Sicily put her phone down as tears burned her gaze. A soft cry left her as the memories washed over her, as if they had just happened moments before. The conversation with her mom had been comical, the two of them fighting over the kind of man Sicily should be looking for.

One minute they were teasing each other and the next her mother stood up, her hand sliding over her heart as a look of fear washed over her pretty face.

Sicily's heart fluttered in her chest remembering the horror of her own screams as her mother dropped to the ground. She was non-responsive and dead before the ambulance could show up. How long had she held her in her lap, singing softly to her, trying to get her to come to? How many prayers had she uttered?

The phone rang and she picked it up, not wanting to answer, but feeling so far beyond alone once again.

"Hey," she whispered into the phone.

"I didn't mean to upset you, Sis. Are you going dancing with the group?"

"No. I can't." She sniffled, not wanting to let Drake know how much she needed someone - anyone to fill up the loss inside of her. Was another person capable of doing that or was she forever damned to suffer?

"I know. I have too much going on to deal with pushy, horny guys and loud, aggressive chicks."

Sicily laughed, a soft snort leaving her. She pressed her hand over her mouth, hating the sound of it. She sounded like the little pig she was.

"I love the sound of your laugh. It's comforting to me." He paused. "Can I come over? I won't stay long. I just... I don't want to be alone right now."

Tears blurred her gaze again, the overly aggressive alpha male on the phone having a very different side to him that she wanted to see firsthand. It scared her like hell to witness it though. It would break her down completely. She needed to fix someone, to belong, to matter, to fill their emptiness. As long as he didn't need that in his life... they were good.

"Yeah. I'd like that."

They hung up and Sicily changed into a pair of sleeping pants and a tank top, not caring at all how she looked. Drake wasn't coming over for a date, but to talk as friends. If they could work on their friendship for a while, she could get in better shape. Once she was healthy and thin maybe things could move into something more. He wouldn't want it before then.

The kiss the other night was just him being a horny male with all his friends hooking up but him. Typical.

She got a glass of tea and made herself a half of a sandwich while she waited on him. Marc and Lisa were gone from the house, the smell of their cologne and perfume filling the place. Sicily breathed in deeply, letting the sensual aromas roll over her. It would feel so damn good to let Drake have her tonight. Just for one night if he wanted a soft place to land. They could make love and then she would send him home, their friends with benefits thing a one-night deal.

The doorbell rang and she spilled her tea on her white shirt, cursing softly as she cleaned it up. She walked to the door and opened it, still wiping at herself.

"Hey. Come on in. I spilled my damn tea. Clumsy fool." She smiled and walked back to the kitchen, ignoring how good he looked.

The dark gray sweats hugged his waist and accentuated every slope of his muscular frame. The white t-shirt he wore left nothing to the imagination. She needed to slow her heart, to douse her hormones in cold water, to chill the fuck out.

"I love tea. I can't remember the last time I let myself have a glass." His voice was rough as if he were lost in thought.

"So is tonight one of those nights you're wanting to let yourself go completely wild and have a glass?" She turned to him and smirked, unable to help herself from teasing him.

"Tell me to go." He took another step toward her, the look on his face almost haunting.

"What?" Sicily set the pitcher and glass down before crossing her arms over her chest. "Why?"

"I came here because I needed the warmth of a woman, Sicily. I want it to be you. I don't want us to move from friends to a one-night stand. Tell me to go." Sadness rushed across his handsome features and she had to stop herself from taking him in her arms and promising him anything he wanted.

"Sit down at the table and tell me what's up with your mom. I'll make you a sandwich and you can indulge in a glass of tea, and then you're going to go. I'm not capable of being anything to you for just one night."

He sat down, running his fingers over his chest and letting out a long painful growl. "I'm so pissed at myself tonight. I need to be in Chicago beside my mother and yet... I left that life so long ago."

Sicily worked to put together a healthy version of a sandwich for him, her hands trembling at the high emotions that ran in the air between them. She wanted to take him to her bed, to kiss him everywhere and make him feel something besides the pain and worry that sat on him. One night would never be enough. She'd not survive that. He had to go.

"Can you not talk to Demetri and have him explain what's going on?"

"No. It's a long story. I'm the only child that doesn't really belong to my Dad. My mother had an affair with my father's best friend and my dad never knew it."

"How do you know that's true?" Sicily set the sandwich down in front of him and poured him a tall glass of tea before sitting down too.

"My real father is a piece of work. He found me and pulled me into his world. He's D's boss now because I pulled my brother into that same world. I didn't know how to survive it without him. Now he's lost in it."

"What world is this that you keep referring to?" Sicily pushed the sandwich closer. "Eat. Please?"

He picked up the sandwich and took a deep bite of it, groaning as he closed his eyes and relaxed in his seat. His pain was almost palpable, the weight of it pressing against her.

"I can't talk about it, Sicily. It's too dangerous." He opened his eyes and moved them across her face and down her body. "Would you do me a favor? It's a lot to ask, but I need it from you so badly."

"I can't, Drake. I'm not that type of woman. One-night stands aren't..."

He cut her off. "No. I need you to stop talking negatively about yourself. I'm going to take Violet's place with you at the gym. I want you to see what I see. I need to watch you fall in love with the beautiful woman that you are again or for the first time. I don't want to fix you. I want to give you a new vision of who you are. Of who I see you are already."

Sicily tried to stop herself, but she couldn't put the brakes on her actions. She moved toward him, sinking down on the floor between his legs and wrapping her arms around his waist. She leaned in and pulled him into a warm hug, wanting to stay there forever.

His arms wrapped around her as his lips pressed to the top of her head. "I need to go or I'm going to stay whether you want me to or not."

"I want you to stay." She moved back and glanced up at him.

He smiled down at her before bending over and brushing his lips by hers. "I want to stay so bad it hurts, but until you need me to stay for you and not to heal me... I can't. You deserve better, and when you're ready... I will be too."

She nodded, melting against him as he tightened his hold on her. This was the first friendship she had ever had that left her panting for far more than friends were granted. She needed his attention and wanted his perspective, but more than anything, she was desperate all of a sudden to heal her heart so he would work to heal his.

Was there really a chance that they could be together? Could she let her guard down just enough to let him in? If he moved into the spot she wanted for him, he was forever stuck. There was no way she was letting him go. Ever.

CHAPTER EIGHT

Sicily jerked up in bed from a nightmare, her skin covered in chill bumps and a light sheen of sweat. She took a shaky breath and pressed her fingers to her eyes, forcing the tears back. How many times would she have to dream of her mother's death only to wake up alone to face the sadness of that one loss all over again?

Drake had finished his sandwich and left after another long hug the night before. He wasn't at all the man she thought him to be, which was good and bad. Thinking of him as a total jerk helped keep her emotions in check, seeing that her hormones were running amuck.

She glanced at the clock and let out a short scream before propelling herself off the bed. She was late. The alarm didn't go off. Tearing through her closet, she tugged down a pair of white pants and a pink top. She slipped sandals on her feet and she was out the door. Kari stopped her before she ran out, the other girl on the phone, her expression serious.

"No. I'll tell her. Sure. Be careful, baby." Kari hung up and released her hold on Sicily. "Jake just called and said someone set fire to Judy's. The roads are blocked off and they've asked all shops to evacuate for the time being."

"Oh no. Was it accidental? Was anyone hurt?" Sicily dropped her purse by the door and walked to the couch, tugging her phone from her pocket as it buzzed.

"He didn't say. We'll go up there in a little while. No need to rush up there now. They won't let you in anyway." Kari shrugged and walked to the kitchen. "Coffee?"

"Yeah." Sicily pressed the talk button on her phone. "This is Sicily."

"Hey, you okay?" Drake.

"Yeah. I actually just woke up. My damn alarm didn't go off." She sighed and ran her fingers through the tips of her hair, trying to pull out a few remaining tangles.

"That's a good thing this morning."

"Are you up there?"

"Yeah. Jake called me in. You need something?"

"Is Martin's truck there by the shop?" She slumped down on the couch, feeling incredibly tired suddenly.

"No. Jake cleared him out. He locked the shop up and headed home. Good kid for sure."

"Yeah, he is. Be careful and text me when I can get back up there."

"I will. I want to talk to you about something today. I'll find you a little later."

"Okay." She almost told him to be careful again, but stopped herself. He was starting to matter a little too much. It was an emotion she couldn't afford. He obviously had feelings for her too, but his seemed more like the need to have someone in his life, not specifically for her. Hers were completely about him. She didn't need anyone filling her time and sucking her energy dry, but for him... it almost seemed like a positive result of sharing in a relationship deeply together.

They hung up and she got up and walked into the kitchen. Kari handed her a steaming mug of coffee, the cream coloring the liquid perfectly. She took a tentative sip and sat down with her friend at the kitchen table.

"Did you guys have fun dancing last night?" Sicily set the cup down and forced herself to relax.

"We did, but we missed you and Drake. You should have come."

"Yeah, I know. We're just dealing with a few things individually, so it was good to have a night off."

"Did he come by and see you?"

"Yeah. How did you know that?"

"Jake forced him to. He's been worried about something lately and Jake said he's not opening up at all about it, not that he's an 'open' kinda guy anyway, but it's gotten worse, like he's retreating into a shell." Kari ran her finger over the rim of her coffee mug. "I guess Jake's just worried. He only has a few friends and I know Drake means a lot to him."

"We talked about some of it, but I'm honestly trying to be careful, Kari. I'm not in a good place in my own life right now. I need to fix all the problems in my own world, with my own health, and then Drake and I can see if there is something between us."

Kari snorted softly, a smile spreading across her pretty face. "Jake and I never would have gotten together if I had to fix myself before we considered it, and... I never would have been fixed without him. He's the reason I'm getting over the pain and rejection of what Frank did. Every day he reminds me how precious I am to him. How much his life means because I'm in it."

Sicily lifted her fingers to her eyes and brushed her tears away. How many tears had her sweet friend cried because of Frank?

Sorry ass bastard.

Jake had started Kari down the road of healing and she had done the same for him.

Maybe it wasn't about getting cleaned up, or thin, or made well before looking for love, but just allowing love to find her in the midst of her messiness. It was the thing that beckoned Jake and Kari to heal - together. Was that the same story aligning for her and Drake?

It was almost too much to hope for.

Kari reached over and patted her hand. "I need to get going. Lisa is showing a house with Marc and I have a shoot at one of the convalescent homes today. Miss Margaret Johnson is turning one hundred."

Sicily smiled and wiped her tears away. "Thanks for the talk. I'm sure we'll figure it out."

"I think you will too. One more thing and I'll leave you alone." Kari squeezed Sicily's shoulder, the look on her face loving concern.

"Sure." Sicily reached up and covered her friend's hand with her own.

"I would rather love a million times and lose than never to have felt the high that love takes you on. Every minute of that bliss is worth all the pain and suffering that comes when something doesn't work out. Take a risk. I know without a doubt that you'll be pleasantly surprised."

"Thanks, Kari." Sicily patted her friend's hand and turned to rest her arms on the table.

She waited until Kari slipped out to pick up the phone and call her brother, Johnny. She hadn't had a chance to talk to him in far too long and just hearing his voice would bring her comfort, no doubt. He was a rock in her life and she in his.

"Hey, Bluebird. How are you?" Her brother's voice brought a smile to her face.

"I'm good. Just sitting at home, waiting for the fire department to clear a fire on the town square where my bakery is."

"Oh no. The bakery didn't get in the way of the flames, right?"

"No. Not that I know of. I just feel really bad for the shop that did catch on fire. The owner is a bitch and a half, but her little elderly mother runs the place. She reminds me of a thin, white version of mom."

Johnny laughed loudly. "Okay... I'm going to leave that one alone. Tell me when you're coming to visit me."

"Maybe over the holidays? I know Kari is hoping that we'll go to Texas, but maybe I can slip away for a few days back at home."

"Yeah, well, New York is only four hours in your car. It's not that far, silly girl."

"Yeah, well, Maine is only four hours in your car. Get in it and let's have dinner tonight." Sicily smirked, loving the opportunity to goad her big brother in any way possible.

"This is true. Tell me what you've been up to. Any man in your life trying to take your time? I could use whooping someone's ass."

Sicily chuckled, knowing good and damn well her brother would love to put a hurting on anyone she dated. He was a miserable father figure in high school and college. Her own father hadn't been a part of their lives since they were younger.

"Actually, the guy who owns a gym here in town seems a little sweet on me, but I'm not too sure about him."

"Does he drive a hog?"

"Yep. That's why I'm thinking I should stay away."

"Oh, hell no. I told you not to date a bike rider. Those bastards are just looking to score."

She laughed again, leaning back and enjoying the moment with her brother. "Not this one. He's quite the gentleman."

"It's a ploy. Don't fall for that shit. We all use it." He laughed again. "Tell me his name so I can call it out loudly when I get into town. I'll challenge him to an old-fashioned ass duel."

"How old are you?" Sicily couldn't help but smile harder.

"Old enough. This playboy got a name?"

"Drake."

"That's trouble right there. Last name?"

"DeMarco. Don't go messing with him either. He's a good man, and we're just friends right now."

"Why does that damn name sound so familiar?"

"No clue. He's not from New York, so it's not like we should know him." Sicily stood up and pulled the phone from her face as it beeped. Martin was calling in.

"Still. It's too familiar. I'm going to do some digging."

"You do that. I have to run. My employee is calling in on the other line. I love you."

"I love you too. Steer clear of Mr. Muscles until I figure out why his name leaves a cold chill down my back."

"Will do, Bro." Sicily hung up and rolled her eyes. Her brother would forever be overprotective. Drake was a simple guy with a rough past, like most men who grew up in Chicago or New York or LA. Big cities always opened up the grand opportunity to get swept up in the sexiness of crime and power. Hell, she would have done the same if her mother hadn't been center stage in her life.

She flipped over to Martin's call. "Hey. You okay? I'm so sorry about not being there this morning. My damn alarm didn't go off."

"I'm good, but the police were there and they want to question us on the fire."

"Us? Why?"

"Because they have us down as suspects seeing that we're the only other bakery in town. Ridiculous, I know."

Sicily let out a long sigh. "Are they wanting to talk to us now? Down at the station or what?"

"They are doing the investigation tonight and tomorrow and then Monday morning first thing we need to be there. I told them I would relay the message."

"That sucks." Sicily rubbed her hand over her stomach, nervousness rising up inside of her. She didn't have anything to hide, but cops made her feel like she was hiding something nevertheless.

"Yeah. The square is closed today, so no worries on coming in. Enjoy your day off and I'll see you after I get out of church tomorrow."

"Okay, kiddo. Thanks for everything." Sicily walked to the kitchen window and glanced out at the beauty afforded them all by fall sweeping in and coloring their world.

"Don't call me that, silly woman. We're only six years apart."
"True. Just call me old lady. Wait... don't you dare."

CHAPTER NINE

Sicily laid around the house for as long as she could, the day turning into afternoon much too slowly. She cleaned every room, including Lisa's, which was a hot mess. Laundry was done and the cabinets in the kitchen were reorganized. She finally resigned herself to going to the gym to waste a few more hours before everyone would be back home. Drake was most likely with Jake wrapping up everything related to the fire and she could just be comfortable in the gym.

No holding in her tummy and trying to breathe through her nose and not pant. Why did the only gym in town have to be owned and operated by the hottest guy in her life? The one she wanted above her at night and wrapped around her in the wee hours of the morning?

Changing into a pair of tight workout pants and a tank top, she stopped by the bathroom mirror and turned her nose up. Getting in shape was going to take forever seeing that she had started to slip again on her diet.

"Get it together," she growled at herself and leaned into the mirror, trying to find something she liked. Her nose was okay. Rolling her eyes, she walked out of the bathroom and grabbed her keys before she changed her mind. The gym was just five minutes up the road. If she saw Drake's truck she would just leave. She wasn't in the mood for batting him off. Today was the type of day where she knew without a doubt that she would just cave in and take a page from Marc and Lisa's book.

The brilliance of the crimson and burnt orange leaves stirred around her feet as she walked into the gym. She paused at the door and bent over, picking up several that had blown in with her.

Violet glanced up from the front desk and chuckled. "Sicily. Leave those there, girl. They are part of the decor this time of year."

"Right? I swear I brought all of them in with me." She paused and looked around the gym while still holding the door.

"He's still downtown. Not sure when he'll be back."

"Oh good. I just need a free day to walk on the treadmill or swim laps. I'm not in the mood for my drill sergeant, though you don't get to tell him that I said that."

Violet acted as if she were zipping her lips. "Not a word."

Sicily smiled and walked to the desk, signing in and picking up a towel. "Thanks."

"Anytime."

The gym was quiet, but it was late afternoon on a Saturday. Most people were curled up on the couch watching the latest football game or sound asleep in the comfort of their beds. She was at the gym, loathing the idea of working up a sweat.

She popped in her ear-buds and got on the nearest machine while mentally coaching herself to get pumped up over working out. A buzz in her ear had her pulling her phone to her face. It was a text from her brother to call him. She started to ignore it until he added the word, 'now' to the next text.

Letting out a long sigh, she dialed his number and glanced up as Drake walked in the front door, blowing in a few leaves of his own. He paused and picked them up, his movements only seeming to bring her attention to the thickness of his shoulders and the curve of his upper arms.

How wicked hot he must look under those clothes.

"Hey. Where did this guy grow up?" Her brother's voice filled the ear-buds.

"Chicago. Are you seriously looking into him? I'm twenty-three, Jon. I don't need you babying me."

"There's a lot of shit on the DeMarcos from Chicago. Looks like they are beyond wealthy, and if I know money, this is dirty money."

"He mentioned having a rough past. Leave it alone, okay?" Sicily whispered into the phone and waved at Drake as he moved toward her. "I have to go."

"Fine, but steer clear of this guy and do me one favor."

"Sure, yeah, okay. What do you want?"

Drake stopped in front of her and nodded toward the phone. She nodded and he started to go, but she reached out and took a hold of the sleeve of his shirt, stopping him and almost falling off the machine.

He reached around it and pressed the stop button as she smiled her thanks.

"Just find out if he's involved in the Castaletta family. They are Chicago-based too. From what I can tell, these two families are deeply intertwined. I'm not good with that, Sis. These Castalettas are bad people, like kill-you-in-an-alley bad."

"What are you saying?" Sicily pressed her ear to the phone.

"I'm saying that if he's involved in the DeMarcos that are linked to the Castalettas, you need to steer clear. He's not on the up and up. We've all heard the stories of these mother fuckers. They are the oldest mob in the US and they don't fuck around. Don't get wrapped up in that. Makes my gang days look like a fairy tale."

"All right fine, but this is ridiculous." She hung up and laid the phone on the machine in front of her before turning her attention to Drake. "Hey."

"Hey. Everything okay?" Drake nodded toward the phone. "Not my business of course."

"Yeah, just my older brother being himself."

"Protective?"

"Insanely so." She laughed, realizing how much she enjoyed him being there. Why was she hoping he wasn't going to be at the gym again? Oh yeah... her wicked tight outfit.

She crossed her arms over herself, but Drake reached up and tugged them back down.

"Don't. You're beautiful. See through my eyes."

She nodded, not quite sure how to answer him. "What happened this morning down at the square?"

"Someone set fire to Judy's. Never in all the years that I've been here have I seen anything like that."

"Was it on purpose?"

"Absolutely. Jake found the remnants of the jar of gas that was wrapped in a t-shirt, lit on fire and thrown through the front window. The blaze started with the curtains up front."

"God that's scary. Any suspects besides me?" Sicily gave a wry smile.

"I'm not sure, but why would you be a suspect?"

"No clue, but Martin called and I'm due down there on Monday morning."

"I'll go with you." Drake reached out and touched the side of her arm.

"You don't need to go with me. I'm a big girl. Like, really big." She laughed and squeezed her hips.

He shook his head. "Don't do that. I like those hips a lot. Don't judge yourself. Everyone else is going to do that enough for us."

"I've been judged my whole life. Seems like if you just get ahead of them and judge yourself, turning it into something humorous, they will leave you alone." She shrugged, not quite sure why she would point out how chunky she was to the one man she wanted in her life.

"I understand completely. I've spent the last ten years of my life running from a past that would leave me without anything in my future should people know it. Being judged is my greatest fear."

"Me too." She glanced down and pressed a few buttons on her phone, not quite sure where the conversation should go from there.

"Have dinner with me tonight?" He slid his hand over the front of the phone. She couldn't help but admire his fingers, her mind taking her down a few paths that would simply leave her needy and willing to break her own rules where he was concerned. How good would it feel to have his fingers wrapped around her hair? Kneading her ass while he took her over and over again.

She glanced up and nodded, her calm destroyed as she panted softly.

"You okay?" He reached up and touched the side of her face. "Don't overdo it on this machine today."

"I'm good." She pulled his hand down, not needing any additional stimuli. "Hey... Can I ask you something personal before you leave me to my grueling workout?"

"Anything."

"You said last night that you weren't actually a DeMarco. That your real father was someone other than Demetri's dad. Who was he?"

Drake glanced around the gym before lifting his gaze to her. "Don't repeat it. Promise me?"

"I promise." She reached out and brushed her fingers down his shoulder, unable to help herself.

"Don't judge me either. You're the one person I want to impress. This isn't impressive."

"Trust me." She squeezed his shoulder softly, her heart aching in her chest for what she knew was coming. The fact that he wanted to impress her shook her to her core.

"My father is a horrible man and he does horrible things. I've been running from him for all of my adult life. My brother D has me finally hidden away. This time it seems to be working."

"Drake. Who is he?"

"Joe Castaletta."

CHAPTER TEN

Sunday was a day of rest, and happened to be the only day Drake DeMarco had off from his beloved gym. It was a lazy day to watch football and lounge around on the couch, wash a few loads of clothes, and eat his one *cheat* meal of the week. Rest was the last thing on his mind when he woke, his stomach a torrent of knots as he tried to walk through what went wrong with his latest obsession.

Something about the look on Sicily's face the day before at the gym told him that she knew more than he wanted her to about who he was before moving to Maine. She'd changed her tune about going to dinner with him and seemed far more interested in running on the treadmill than giving him another second in her presence.

"Weird," he grunted and got out of bed. Being a bachelor had been a necessity for a while, the need to ensure that he was safe in Maine had left him lonely. She was the first girl in five years who hadn't been a planned one night stand in another town over just to release some of the overload of testosterone that burst through him on a regular basis.

"And... she wants shit nothing to do with you," he grumbled and pulled on a pair of old sweats before walking into the kitchen. The house was on the outskirts of town in the woods, the privacy it afforded was well worth dealing with the fixer-upper state it was in.

Drake groaned again and poured himself a cup of coffee before flipping through the paper that lay on the table from the day before. The fire in the town square was on the front page and Margaret Smith, the owner of Judy's, stood in front of the heap of rubble that was her store, looking dejected. Her mother stood next to her, the elderly woman in tears over the loss of her hobby, her passion, her job.

"Good play, Margaret," Drake scoffed and took a sip of his coffee. Something wasn't right about the fire, but then again the owner of Judy's bakery never seemed to be on the up and up. Having lived the life of a villain for far too long, he knew one when he saw one.

He pressed his finger over the pretty woman's face and rubbed it. "You, my dear, are most certainly a villain."

The weather was perfect for a long run, but going at it alone just didn't sound like fun. Worry over his mother pressed against him and the sickening feeling that he was losing the battle with Sicily didn't help. Being around someone else for a little while would help stave off the fear that forever would be spent like the last five years – alone.

The demons of his past seemed to wait around every corner to threaten his future –

and Sicily seemed to have gotten a whiff of them somehow.

Probably for the better.

He was way more interested in her than she was in him. The thick curve of her rear, the fullness of her breasts and slim waist left his body hardening every time he even began to think of her. The fact that she wanted to lose weight was almost something to lament over. She was at her perfect size, which was so much healthier than the frail looking thing that had showed up in Bar Harbor a few months before.

Why women beat themselves up for having luscious curves and a little extra meat on their bones was something he would never figure out, but where he didn't understand it, he wanted to help her. If only she would let him.

"That shit isn't happening." He picked up his phone and dialed his only friend in Maine.

"Hey, buddy," Jake answered on the first ring.

"Hey. What's on your plate today?"

"Two egg whites and grilled turkey. You?"

Drake chuckled. "I take it you're lying, or Kari's with the girls and you're getting your first healthy meal of the week."

"I'm lying. I always do when you ask about my diet. I figure it's all going to catch up to me soon."

"Sooner than you want." Drake ran his fingers through his hair. "It's nice outside. You wanna catch a long run with me?"

"Absolutely. I'm meeting up with Kari later today, but I got a few hours. Where you wanna go?"

"How about around the harbor? I could use the scenery."

"Yeah, sounds great. Dress warm. The wind's already blowing like crazy."

"Gotcha. I'll meet you at the doc on Twelfth and Jones."

"See you there."

Drake set the phone down, hesitating over whether to text Sicily or not. Being a stalker wasn't at the top of his list of things to do, but it would be nice to let her know he was thinking of her. Their kiss on the back porch a few days back left him panting for more. So much more.

The night in the kitchen when she let him hold her was bliss and yet... "So fucking fleeting. Why?"

Letting out a long growl, he dropped the internal banter, no better at encouraging himself than the beautiful girl who had stolen his heart months ago. Too bad she didn't realize it and probably never would with the way things were going.

The weather was beyond blissful as Drake drove his bike to the harbor, the wind chilly and refreshing. He parked and locked it up as Jake got out of his old truck.

"I'm thinking I need to get me one of those." Jake nodded to the motorcycle.

"Oh yeah? Gets the girls every time." Drake wagged his eyebrows and stood, stretching his arms to the heavens and twisting his torso.

"I got the girl. It's your turn now." Jake popped him in the back and nodded to the sidewalk that stretched around the string of shops. "Good thing it's Sunday or this wouldn't be possible without having to dodge old ladies and baby strollers."

Drake laughed and walked to the sidewalk with Jake. "Jumping over a stack of old ladies holding baby strollers would be easier than getting the girl. She's damn near impossible."

"You still have your eye on Sicily?" Jake nodded as they picked up their pace, jogging at an aggressive speed.

It would be good to bleed out some of his angst through his sweat glands. Pumping iron for the afternoon might help as well, but he wasn't sure if he could force himself to stay busy and not hit her up again for dinner. Rejection was assured, but it didn't matter. He would subtly push until she told him to go away for good. She'd have to mean it, too, which she didn't just yet.

"I can't seem to take my eyes off of her. She's fucking with my sleep, my moods, my eating, my workouts. I sound like a high school girl with a crush."

"You sound like you've fallen in love with a girl who has no idea you have feelings for her."

"She knows. I'm sure she knows." Drake pushed forward a little more as Jake grunted next to him.

"Tell me how she knows."

"Just little things, man. I think she thought I wanted a project in her, like some girl I could take to the gym and fix up, but that's not at all what I want. I think I've made that clear. I kissed her the other night on the porch out at their house, but she didn't seem too happy about that."

"Maybe she's not interested." Jake shrugged.

"Maybe, but I can't shake her." Drake let out a long sigh and tried to let his thoughts dissipate.

"We'll call Kari when we get back to the dock and get the lowdown."

"Sounds good." Drake glanced out at the water, the surface appearing like a polished sheet of glass. "I'm a little concerned about the situation down at Judy's, too."

"Oh yeah? How so?"

"Why is Sicily being called in tomorrow to the police station? Seems a little shady to me."

"It's just standard procedure. They'll call in anyone who had suspicion sitting on them. Sicily is the only other baker in town and they sit right across from each other. I wouldn't think anything of it."

"I'm going with her." Drake glanced over, his sense of trepidation high where the situation was concerned. Something wasn't right, and if Sicily was involved, he would be, too. Whether she wanted his help or not. He'd pull the fucking friend card ten times a minute to shut her down over him being there if needed.

"I think that's a great idea. You should represent her if she'll let you. She's been through a lot this year. Her mom passed in January or February, I believe. They were really close and Kari said she's had a really hard time with it. She's got a lot of fear in her due to the suddenness of her mom's heart attack."

"Yeah. She mentioned it. I'm all for someone getting healthy, but she's too hard on herself. I hate that she thinks she's fat. She's fucking hot to me."

"She is a beautiful girl. Exotic and feminine."

"Back off." Drake laughed and winked as they turned the far corner of the harbor and pivoted to head back.

"No worries, brother. I'm head over heels with my girl. I'm going to pop the question at Christmas this year. We're going to Texas and Kari's wanting everyone to come with us. You think you'd be down?"

"Yeah. Just depends on what happens with Sicily. I'm not going down there as a fifth wheel or something worse if things don't pan out. I asked her out again last night and she turned me down." He shrugged as if it wasn't that big of a deal, which it wasn't. Persistence was the key. The spark was there, of that he was assured. He just had to figure out how to blow it into a full-force fire.

"It'll work out. I've seen the way she looks at you." Jake slowed a little and Drake pulled back with him.

They jogged at a slower pace for the next hour, making small talk about the town and upcoming football season. Some part of him wanted to be involved in sports with the local kids like Jake was, but the gym took up too much of his time. When he wasn't helping clients with their fitness, he picked up a case or two as a freelance lawyer, his brother forcing him to get his degree when he was younger, though it almost killed him.

The gym was his mainstay and where it did really well. There wasn't pressure by the force of competition to be the best in town. His was the only gym. Sicily had to push to make sure the people of Bar Harbor knew how good her treats were. Her competition was right across the road... or was.

I'd love to sample her treats. All of them.

"Alright, boss. I can't do another one. I gotta shower and get over to Kari's place. They're having burgers this afternoon for some of Lisa's clients and I'm the chef."

"Where's Marc?"

"He's headed back already. Left this morning."

"Fuck. I don't know how he's doing that long-distance thing."

"I guess when you don't have a choice, you just do what you gotta do. He loves Lisa and she calms that part of him that wants to hump anything with an available hole." Jake snorted and pulled out his phone. "You want me to call Kari about Sicily?"

"Nah. We'll figure it out. I'm gonna take a few more laps and work through some of this shit."

"I'm here if you need me, man."

"Get outta here. Making me feel all emotional and shit." Drake turned and jogged off, a smile brushing over his lips as Jake's voice lifted up behind him.

"I love you, man!"

His response was a chuckle as he lifted the bird in the air.

CHAPTER ELEVEN

Sunday was a waste, a day to lie in the bed and lament over the truth about Drake. He was part of the DeMarco-Castaletta clan, and Sicily's brother had been serious about his warning. Some part of her wanted to call and find out the full details on what it could mean, but knowing anything too damning would completely snuff out hope. Hope that she and Drake might become something when she lost her weight and he, what... stopped being a villain?

She woke on Monday morning to the alarm, her desire to get up and do anything officially gone. It would have been a good day to get back in the kitchen and experiment a little, but she was due at the police station at eight. How they had her down as a suspect was beyond her, but she would push past her angst and answer their questions. Things would get cleared up and she could get back to her life.

"Some life it is," she grumbled and milled through her clothes.

Drake saw her differently than she saw herself, his words telling her as much, but it was more about the way his eyes moved across her, the heat in his gaze almost searing her. Seemed odd for a guy who sold fitness to be interested in someone who wasn't at all fit, but squishy and out of shape?

Tugging a black sweater out of the closet, she pulled it over her head and grabbed a pair of jeans to go with it. Heels and a little bit of make-up and she was out the door. She'd have to change before going into the bakery, but her appearance might help a little with the interview at the station. She ran her fingers around the top of her jeans as she walked to the car, noticing that there was a little extra room in them.

"Seems like almost dying at the gym is the answer to the problem." She smirked and got into her compact car. It was the perfect weather to leave the windows down, but showing up at the police station with windblown hair might give them the idea that she was wild and reckless. She was anything but.

A quick trip down the street and two right turns and she was there. Bar Harbor was so different from New York, the distance from here to there always nothing more than a few minutes. To get anywhere in New York you had to give yourself an hour or more depending on the time of day.

She got out of the car and stopped short as Drake nodded at her. He was leaned against a handicap sign, his bike sitting locked up just behind him.

"Hey. You look good." He moved toward her and stopped short just before reaching her.

She held her breath, scared that he might reach out and pull her into a hug. Seeing him was bad enough, but having to drag him deep into her lungs would likely melt her resolve where he was concerned.

His slacks fit him all too well and the tight black T-shirt was the perfect complement to his attire. He looked like sex incarnate, which wasn't at all something she needed to focus on. She was being interviewed as part of a federal crime.

Get it together. He's a criminal or mobster. You're not getting involved. No matter what.

"Hey. What're you doing here? Get a parking ticket for stealing handicapped spots?"

He chuckled and moved in beside her as she walked to the door. He opened it and she walked into the station, her concern over the interview to come almost squelched thanks to the increased flooding of hormones over the dark scent of his cologne that assaulted her.

"Funny, girl, you are." He moved up beside her as she stopped at the front desk.

"I'm good, Drake. I don't need you here with me." She turned as the clerk spun around in her chair and smiled up at them. Sicily ignored the soft growl from the handsome man beside her and focused on the girl.

"I'm Sicily Moretti. I was summoned for a questioning this morning?"

"On the fire at Judy's?" The girl lifted her eyebrow and let her eyes move over Sicily before turning to Drake. The girl had to be wondering what the hell the town hottie was doing with the town baker. A fat baker at that.

"Yeah," Sicily mumbled and pulled out her phone, flipping through it to make sure she had her time right.

Drake shifted beside her as if he were uncomfortable. He should be. Monsters and cops didn't mix.

"I gotcha right here. Just have a seat over there and we'll have Detective Brown bring you back shortly. Is this your lawyer?"

"Yep," Drake responded before she could.

She didn't deny it simply because looking like they were trying to pull something over on the cops wouldn't go over well. Sicily gave the woman a tight smile and nodded before turning and walking to the waiting room. He sat next to her and leaned back. He picked up the paper next to him and started to read it.

Sicily popped it down as anger raced over her.

Drake glanced up and winked at her before picking up the paper again.

Ass.

"What do you think you're doing?" she whispered angrily.

"I'm reading the paper. Do you want to read it? If so, just ask." He chuckled and pulled it down. "How are you more beautiful when you're angry? It should be a crime."

"Not funny. You're not a lawyer. You own the town gym. Everyone knows that. The cop is going to know that, so what the hell are you doing?" She hated the pissy sound of her voice, but the combination of needing him and not wanting to need him raged inside of her, threatening to spill over and ruin her composure.

He set the paper down before moving forward, his actions putting him closer than she wanted. "I'm a lot of things, Sicily. You don't know me and you're judging my abilities. Don't. I don't judge yours."

She turned as the girl called her name. "Miss Moretti. You and your lawyer can come this way."

"Thank you," Sicily called out a little too brightly. She glanced back at Drake as he stood and moved up beside her. "This conversation isn't over."

"Good. I wanted to take you to lunch anyway." Drake smiled and pressed his hand to the small of her back as they walked through the door near the reception area.

"I'm taking Martin out for a well-deserved hamburger," she barked and tried to still her beating heart. There was no way in hell that Drake had a law degree. He was blowing smoke and acting like a punk-ass teenaged boy. He might be interested in something with her, but the more she got to know him, the less she was.

Do you really know anything about him or are you just assigning a past and a personality to him?

She sighed, trying to let go of her thoughts as the receptionist showed her to a small room with a single table and white walls. Sicily walked in and took a seat, her attention moving off of Drake quickly and onto the situation before her. The door closed and she glanced over to him.

"I didn't do this. Why am I here?"

His expression softened from cocky to concern. "It's all going to be okay. Just let me talk and you just respond when I look at you, okay?"

"Do you have a law degree or are we blowing smoke up the local police force's asses together? I don't want to be part of anything under the table. I'm a good person."

He flinched at her last words and she regretted them immediately. He was a good person, too. His comment at the restaurant the other day about his ideal woman washed over her. He wanted someone who could see past his scars to love him, to see that, even though he might never be great, he was trying hard to be good.

The door opened and a cop in a white button down, black slacks, and a red tie walked in. His smile lifted as he turned his attention to Drake.

"Mr. DeMarco. I didn't realize this was a case you'd be on." He extended his hand and the men spoke for a minute as Sicily's heart dropped.

He was a lawyer. How? When? Sickness rolled over her as she realized that she didn't know anything about Drake. How ignorant of her to think he was simply a one-dimensional cookie-cutter meathead. She hated to be judged and here she was doing it to the one guy she wanted.

The cop turned to her and took a seat, pulling out a handful of pictures.

"I just need you to answer a few questions this morning, Miss. Moretti."

"Of course," Sicily muttered and turned her gaze to Drake, who seemed to be ignoring her now.

Perfect. Exactly what I needed today.

"See this dark blue cardigan?"

Sicily leaned over and looked at the picture, the cardigan a snapshot from a sales magazine. "Yeah. Sure."

"Do you have one like this?" He lifted his eyebrow as she glanced up at him.

"May I?" She hesitated before picking up the photo. She needed a closer look.

He smiled and nodded as Drake leaned in closer. The sexy aroma of his soap and skin rolled over her and she glanced at him as if warning him to back the hell up.

"Yes. I have one like this. It's at my shop."

"You sure about that?" the cop asked and took the picture before showing a few more.

"Don't answer that." Drake leaned forward and pulled the picture toward them. He glanced up. "Paul, I was at the fire that day. The evidence of what was used to set the place on fire could not have survived."

"I agree, but that doesn't mean we don't have a few things that place your client in the shop just before the fire."

"What?" Sicily yelled, her emotions going from calm to full-blown panic.

"Did you know that the old woman who runs the shop has been put in the hospital?" The cop turned back to Sicily as the reality of the situation rolled over her.

They believe I did it.

"Unrelated," Drake barked. "Stick to your questions or we'll be leaving."

"Right." Paul sat back and tapped on his pad of paper. "Where were you on Saturday?"

"At the gym, with Drake and his staff." Sicily nodded toward him as numbness started to wash over her. Judy was in the hospital and her bitch of a daughter was probably laughing her head off. Where Sicily wasn't willing to play nefarious games, a healthy level of competition had been part of the fun between them. There was nothing Sicily wouldn't do for Judy, the bakery's namesake and the sweet elderly woman, who was in the hospital now.

"All day?" The cop leaned forward and glanced toward Drake.

"I was at home sleeping. Had lunch with my roommates, worked out, and went back home after that."

"Got an alibi for Saturday morning at three?"

"I was asleep."

"Were your roommates at the house then?" He leaned in and Sicily sat back, suddenly overwhelmed. Tears burned her gaze and she shook her head.

"I guess. As I said, I was asleep. I would never hurt anyone. I'll get the cardigan from the shop and show it to you. I care about Judy, and am headed to the hospital to check on her now that I know." The tears spilled over and Drake took charge of the conversation.

"Charge her with something or ask your questions and make it brief. My client's been through a lot lately." Drake patted the table.

Paul nodded. "We have a little more to do and then we'll revisit with you. No need to look for the sweater. It was in Judy's and is part of our evidence."

He picked up a bag from the floor and dropped it on the table.

The room spun and Sicily took a shallow breath, unsure of what to say or do.

"Could belong to anyone. DNA test it and call us." Drake stood, reaching down and pulling Sicily up. "Come on, Miss Moretti. We're done here."

Sicily nodded and walked out into the hall with Drake's arm around her back. They reached the front door and he pushed it open before pulling her to the side.

"How do they have that sweater? Is it yours? Do you need to tell me something?"

"No. I'll get mine. I wouldn't... never mind." She jerked from him as a sob left her.

They didn't believe her.

He didn't believe her.

Fuck all of it.

CHAPTER TWELVE

Drake let out a long sigh as he parked at the gym and locked up his bike. The look on Sicily's face said that she assumed the worst from him – again. He was simply trying to get her to help him figure out why the fuck the sweater was at Judy's. He wasn't insinuating anything. The girl had brothers. She had to know that most men who wanted to say something would just say it.

First her thinking that he was continuously poking at her weight and not that she was a criminal.

"So fucking ridiculous," he growled and dropped the chain the bike. A soft grasp resounded behind him and he realized how loud he had been with his cursing. The Beltmans were walking out of the gym and stopped in their tracks. "I'm so sorry."

"It's all right, son." Mr. Beltman reached out and patted Drake on the shoulder. "Something got you stirred up?"

He glanced to Mrs. Beltman with a look of apology on his face and nodded. "Yeah. The girl of my dreams is quickly becoming a nightmare."

"Drop her ass," Mr. Beltman grumbled and huffed.

"Frank. Watch your language." She glanced at Drake. "You say the word fuck and he thinks he can start ranting and raving like a sailor again. Did you tell him you were a sailor, honey?"

"He did." Drake laughed and moved to the door, turning around and smiling. "Sorry again, guys. I appreciate you letting me slide this time."

"Do you love her?" the older man barked out.

"I think so." Drake glanced down and hoped like hell they were the only ones hearing the conversation. He didn't feel up to explaining himself to anyone else right now.

"Then fight through it. Over-communicate, I always say."

"You do not." Mrs. Beltman popped him again. "All sailors are liars. You hear me?"

Drake laughed and waved, slipping into the gym before they could start on him again. They were good people, and just seeing them lifted his mood a bit. He glanced up and nodded at Violet and Jasmine before making a beeline to the small office he had set up for himself near the back of the gym.

Everything with Sicily would work out one way or the other. The old man was right. He just had to communicate more and keep pushing as much as she would let him. He closed his door and dropped down into his chair before pulling out his phone. A quick text wouldn't hurt anything.

Drake: *What if... just what if... my question earlier was to try and get you to join my team in solving this mystery? What if I'm actually a pretty decent guy and the type that says exactly what he means? Like, no mincing words or any of that shit? What if you just don't know me well enough yet? Sicily... what if?*

She didn't answer right away and he re-read his text before dropping the phone on his desk and leaning back. He brushed his hands over his face as the image of her at the station rolled over him. Her tight dark blue jeans were stretched across her ass and fit so well it was sickening. Those heels she wore drove desire to the center of his gut, her legs thin and fit just like he liked them.

He brushed his hand down the front of his slacks, trying to think back to the last time he made love to a woman. It had to have been since before meeting her. He couldn't fathom going to another town for a one-night stand after starting to have feelings for the wayward baker.

"Fuck. Why do you have to be so damn difficult?"

The phone buzzed and he jumped up like his ass was on fire, his heart skipping a beat in his chest. He had it bad. This wasn't good at all. Picking up his phone, he checked it and it was a text from Demetri to get the blue phone out.

"This can't be good." Drake moved to his file cabinet and unlocked it before pulling out a bright blue phone D had given him the last time they were together. It was encrypted and allowed only the two of them to pick up on it. The reminder of his past life caused him to suffer a full-body shiver. Things were so much better than they used to be. Death and the threat of dismemberment always lurked around every corner in his younger years. He'd take girl problems any day over what used to keep him up at night and haunt his dreams.

"Hey." D picked up on the first ring.

"Hey yourself, brother. What's going on?" Drake locked the door to his office and sat back down. The situation with Sicily would have to wait a little while. If D was calling... something was wrong.

"Mom's not doing good, man. I want you to come home and see her before she passes."

Drake rubbed his chest absently as sadness washed over him. "Fuck, man. I knew this was going to be bad news. You never call with anything but shitty news."

D laughed, but the sound fell flat. "I'll work on that. This weekend, Drake."

"That bad?" Drake closed his eyes and shoved the need to cry as far down in his belly as he could manage.

"Really bad. She's asking for you and everyone thinks she's nuts."

"I bet. She thinks I'm dead, D. Like all of them do."

"Nah, bro. I told her that you were just hidden really well to keep you away from Joe."

"Fuck, D. You know she could murmur that stuff and have me caught. I'd never live to tell about it if my dad knew I was hiding from him and his shit."

"She's so out of it that no one would believe her. Come here and Izzy and I will come get you, Drake. Flight is on Friday afternoon and you can fly back out Sunday. I'll have the boys set up a special time for you to come in and visit her."

"You can keep the visit under wraps from everyone?" Drake looked up as worry tugged at him. How good would it be to see his mother before she passed?

"Yeah. Trust me."

"I always have. Can I bring someone with me?"

"You got a girl finally?" Demetri chuckled as Drake shook his head.

"Fuck you."

"Not my type, pretty boy."

"Yeah, your type's been ignoring you for the last twenty years." Drake's turn to laugh.

"Alright. I'm gonna getcha ass for that one." D laughed again. "Tickets will be on your other phone in a few minutes. I'll send two. The girl know about all of us?"

"Sort of. She knows all she needs to know for now."

"Hmmm... sounds serious."

"Yeah, speaking of. I gotta go. I'll see you later this week. Tell momma to hang on for me."

"Will do. Stay safe."

Drake stood and turned the phone off before dropping it back into the middle drawer of his filing cabinet. He locked it and walked back to the desk, the ding coming from his regular phone most likely the tickets. There was a slim chance Sicily would go with him to Chicago on a whim, but if there was one thing that would entice her, it would be to find out more about his past.

His mention of being Joe's boy on Saturday and her reaction told him that she or someone close to her had been digging. He needed to ask her to stop. It was far too dangerous for all of them, especially him.

He grabbed his phone and walked back out into the gym. "I'm out for a while. Don't let the place go to hell."

"Already has," Violet called after him.

"Ah, then never mind. You're fired."

The girl's laughing at him caused him to smile. If only Sicily could see a version of him that included the fun-loving guy he could be when life was a little settled. Maybe that's what he needed to do. Focus on showing her the side of himself that she hadn't really taken notice of yet.

Flowers. Dinner. Sex.

Definitely sex.

Nerves tore up his center as he walked up to the shop and turned. Her car wasn't in the parking lot.

"Shit." He pushed the door open as Martin looked up from the register and smiled. The place was empty because it was so close to closing time.

"Hey, Mr. DeMarco. How are you, sir?"

"Good, Martin. Your bossy boss here?" He lifted the flowers. "If not, I gotcha something."

Martin laughed and shook his head. "No, sr. She's been off today because of all of the police drama this morning."

"Did you guys get to go to lunch?"

"We did. Great food, but the company was awesome." Martin picked up a towel and adverted his eyes as his cheeks colored a little.

The kid had a crush on Sicily. It was almost comical. He was what? Seventeen?

"So you're a senior this year?"

"Sure am. I'm getting ready to head to New York after graduation. I got into NYU. I plan to own my own bakery like Sicily someday. Might even come back here and see if she's ready for a partnership." He wagged his eyebrows.

The kid was egging Drake on. He had to be.

"Interesting. I don't think I know your family, do I?" Drake leaned against the counter and eyed the kid, something about him a little unnerving.

"Sure you do. It was my Aunt Margaret's shop that got burned down. Judy is my Grandma." He shrugged and started to clean again.

Drake stiffened. "Why the hell aren't you working over there, then?"

"They didn't have an opening. My grandma keeps me pretty busy with her yard and stuff, but they don't take my passion for baking seriously."

"Hmmmm... Does Sicily know that?"

"I don't know. Wasn't part of the interview. There's no need to do a family background check on the guy who's rolling your buns and basting your pastries." He glanced up and locked his gaze on Drake's.

This kid's outta his fucking mind. Why hadn't I noticed before?

Drake nodded and walked to the door. "Alright, well have fun rolling and basting. I'm going to get the girl. Later, kid."

He walked out and got on his bike. Something was fucked up with the situation and only Sicily could be the judge of how to handle it. He would hit her up with it and the hopes of scoring a date the next day. Her not answering his text meant she wasn't willing to listen today, but he could wait.

CHAPTER THIRTEEN

She still hadn't answered his text from the day before. The honest truth of it was that she didn't know how to. Tugging on her yoga pants and leaning over her bed, she pulled the text up again.

Drake: *What if... just what if... my question earlier was to try and get you to join my team in solving this mystery? What if I'm actually a pretty decent guy and the type that says exactly what he means? Like, no mincing words or any of that shit? What if you just don't know me well enough yet? Sicily... what if?*

"Yeah, what if?" she grumbled and fell forward, flopping down on her bed accidentally. A growl left her and she rolled on her back before throwing her legs in the air and trying to wiggle into the pants.

Lisa stopped by the door and snorted. "Um, you need some help?"

"Go away. I'm trying to get these on and someone washed them in hot water."

"They're yoga pants, Sis. They are supposed to look like someone painted them on you."

"Then never mind." Sicily ripped them from the middle of her thighs where they were stuck and tossed them across the room. She sat up and let out a long sigh. "Do you think men say things that hint around what they really mean?"

"Um, yeah, you're going to have to reword that and say it again." Lisa laughed and walked to where the pants were crumpled on the floor, picking them up and stopping in front of the bed as she rolled one of the legs up tight. "Give me your foot. I'll show you the art to these."

Sicily lifted her foot, not willing to fight over it. "So like if I said to you, 'Those pants look good. They make you look slim,' would you think I'm simply saying you look good, or thank God for those pants because your fat ass looks horrid in everything else."

Lisa glanced up and lifted her eyebrow. "You sound fucking mental. Girls beat around the bush and add hidden meaning to everything. Men say it like it is. If Marc says I look good, I look good. If he says he wants tacos, he's not feeling me out to see if I want steak."

Sicily nodded and lifted her other foot as Lisa worked the pants up her leg. "I guess I expect Drake to judge me any minute about my weight."

"That's because you judge yourself." Lisa shrugged. "When I thought I was a lesbian in high school, my mom and dad tried to be cool about it. They grounded me over my grades and sneaking out of the house, but I remember turning everything back to blame them for doing those things because I was gay. It had nothing to do with me being gay and everything to do with me sneaking out of the fucking house. I did that because I knew at any minute they were going to start belittling me and punishing me simply for a life choice. You're doing that to yourself now. No one is judging you, but you're blaming them for doing it just in case it starts. Stop. It's dumb."

"You went through a lesbian spell in high school? Why didn't you tell me?"

"Because you were my girl crush." Lisa shoved the pants up high and winked. "Hey, baby. How you doin'?"

Sicily laughed and swatted her with a pillow before getting up and trying to chase after her as she bolted. "These damn pants are stuck on my thighs again."

Lisa paused by the door and smiled. "What lovely thighs they are."

Sicily rolled her eyes and bent over, jerking at them and jumping until they were on. Why anyone would put themselves through the torture of wearing tight-fitting yoga pants was beyond her, until she looked in the mirror.

"Oh, my God. These make me look slim." She smiled and turned the other way. "I love these things."

"Told ya!" Lisa yelled from down the hall. "Just don't wear them too long."

"Why? I love them."

"They cut off circulation."

Sicily chuckled and walked to the closet, changing shirts and putting on tennis shoes before grabbing her phone and heading to the kitchen. "I'm headed to the gym. You want to go with me?"

"No, but when are you going to the shop? You've been leaving Martin there a lot lately."

"Yeah, I know. He's such a great kid and so much help." Sicily picked up her keys. "I'm going to work out and then I'm going in. I wanted to play racquetball today, but I don't have a partner. You up for it?"

"Um no. Does this look like a racquetball body?" Lisa ran her hands down her perfect body.

"Yes, actually it does." Sicily laughed and walked to the door. "Wish me luck."

"On what?"

"On whooping Drake's ass."

"You're going to get him to play with you?"

"Sure, why not?" She didn't wait for the answer, but slipped out into the mid-fall morning. The hint of burning leaves and chilly weather left her feeling fully alive. Lisa was right on her assessment of the situation. Sicily was waiting for the other shoe to fall and preparing for the worst.

It was unfair to everyone, especially Drake. She got in the car and pulled out her phone, texting him.

Sicily: *What if... just what if I'm the girl who was never good enough? What if I was the one who struggled with my weight? With death and depression? What if you seem too good to be true? What if I'm scared that letting you in a little would leave me open and bare to devastation when you determined there was a better what if?*

He responded immediately, the ding on her phone causing her to jump.

Drake: *What if risking something meant gaining everything? Come to me and let's talk.*

Sicily*: No talking. I'm coming to work out. Play racquetball with me.*

Drake: *You like getting spanked?*

Sicily: *Only in the bedroom.*

Drake: *That's not fair. Vixen.*

Sicily: *What if...*

She laughed and dropped the phone in her purse before pulling out onto the quiet streets outside of their neighborhood. It was nice not to fight traffic or hordes of people. Now if she could get her name cleared from being the town villain, she'd be good. Good thing she knew a senior counsel defense attorney.

"I wonder if he takes payment for services in any currency other than dollars." She laughed and parked at the gym, putting her nefarious thoughts away. She needed to be careful where he was concerned. The texts were enough teasing for one day. Maybe...

Nervousness rose up in her as she approached the door, but she pushed past it. A playful friendship would be the starting point. She would have to work on not assuming everything he said had some hidden meaning to it, but she would. She could start that part of the journey immediately.

He glanced up from the front desk as she walked in, the smile on his handsome face almost melting her.

"I thought you might be teasing me."

"About playing today?"

"About the bedroom." He winked and picked up the phone next to him. "Vi. You're needed at the front."

"Now look," she moved toward him and pressed her arms to the desk between them, "you have to go easy on me. It's been years since I've played."

"Not happening. I don't know how to go easy. I'm a hard hitting, competitive bastard. I thought you knew this." He smiled and nodded toward his office. "I'll grab us some racquets."

Violet waved as she walked up. "Those yoga pants are to die for. Where did you get them?"

"Back in New York. They were a bitch to get on. I had to get help." Sicily laughed and turned in time to catch Drake's eyes roll across her.

"Well worth the effort. I'll volunteer my help anytime." He licked at his lips absently and ducked into this office.

"Um, wow." Violet leaned against the counter. "Are you guys dating now?"

"No. Just friends." Sicily rubbed at her neck as heat rolled over her. Maybe flirting with him wasn't such a good idea. She could be subtle about it, but he had gone from zero to full blast in twenty seconds.

"I want a friendship like that." She turned and laughed. "Be careful with his heart, please. He hasn't been flirty with a woman in this place in all the years I've known him. Something's up and if you hurt him..."

"You'll come after me?" Sicily lifted her eyebrow as she forced a smile. She couldn't shake Violet's comment. Drake hadn't been flirty with anyone in the gym in the last five years? That seemed like a stretch.

"Gently so, but yes. Now... go kick his ass and take away his bragging rights please..."

Drake walked up and rolled his eyes. "Please. I haven't lost a game, any game, since I was a kid. This is just a friendly game so I can get some exercise and Sicily can fill me in on her day."

Sicily laughed and walked away, looking over her shoulder and once again caught him checking her out. "Come on and stop staring at my pants. I know they're tight."

He moved up beside her. "Nope. You don't get to do that. For the next hour I'm going to bless you by telling you everything I'm thinking and feeling. You don't get to assign words to my expressions or actions. Sound good?"

"Do I really want to hear what you're thinking in your head?" She laughed and he opened the door to the racquetball court.

"Probably not, but my thoughts are much better than what you're giving me credit for." He shrugged and dropped the racquets before pulling his keys and cards from his pockets. He tugged his shirt over his head and Sicily turned to face the wall in front of her.

"So what were you thinking a minute ago about my fat ass in these horribly tight yoga pants?" Her voice was much too high and tight. The sight of him half naked almost did her in.

He spoke softly, his mouth so close to her ear that his warm breath skittered across her skin. "I was thinking that the pants look beautiful on you, but they pull in too many of your assets. If I could just see you in your natural state to assess how magnificent you really are, things would be easier."

"In my panties?" She jerked her head around and took a step back. "Your serve."

"Ladies first." He winked and handed her the ball. "Not your panties... jeez."

She let out a long breath and held up her racquet, getting ready for his attack.

"In your shower." He hit the ball and she moved toward it, her heart racing before her first step was taken.

CHAPTER FOURTEEN

She was beyond fine as she stood there in front of him, wanting to play ball, but more concerned with how she looked than anything else. His plan was to be totally open and honest with her. She wanted in? She was getting in... as far and as fast as she would allow herself to.

He wasn't playing entirely fair as he flung his saucy comments at her, but nothing was ever fair in love and war. She hit the ball hard, surprising him and pulling him out of his meanderings.

"And what would you be doing in the shower while checking out my assets?" Her voice carried behind her, her pretty face and resulting expressions from the conversation hidden to him.

"Washing your back, of course." He hit the ball again – hard.

She moved toward the front wall, letting the small blue ball ricochet off the back wall. It came right to her. With a gentle tap, it hit the front wall and rolled.

Her point. *Fuck.*

He had to change the subject. Getting her naked in the shower wasn't a topic of conversation he could maintain and keep his head on straight. His cock had taken note of her the minute she had come into the gym, and was at a full erection now, the big ass thing poking him in the stomach as if in reminder. He adjusted himself and let out a soft puff of air.

"Have you heard anything from the station yet?" He moved up as she looked up and smiled. Her eyes were filled with competitiveness and it caused something inside of him to tighten.

Mine. I need her to be mine.

She hit the ball and moved out of his way as he jogged toward it, hitting it back easily.

"I haven't heard back from them. I figure I will soon." She moved up beside him, hitting the ball again and brushing her arm by his. "Thank you for coming as my legal defense. I'll pay you for your time."

"Just go with me to dinner soon."

"That sounds incestuous."

"Nah. It's just food. It's when I ask you to get in the shower with me... then it'll get a little sticky." He hit the ball hard again and she faltered, their conversation finally seeming to bother her. She missed and it was his point. He let out a victory holler as she dropped her racket and turned on him, walking with anger in her gaze.

It was about to get interesting.

"You did that shit on purpose. That wasn't fair, Drake." The saucy Italian woman had curves like something out of eighteenth century porn, her dark silky hair and warm brown eyes doing the rest of the trick.

Drake reached for her, turning them both and pinning her against the wall as he moved in like a snake on the attack. The kiss was hard and filled with every ounce of passion he had for her. She pushed against him at first, but melted the minute his tongue slipped into her mouth.

The moan that left her undid him completely. He ran his hands from her face, over her shoulders, and down to her hips before grabbing her luscious ass and picking her up. He pressed her to the wall and ground into her before breaking the kiss.

"No, baby. This is unfair." He rolled his hips again and sucked her lip into his mouth as she watched him with hooded eyes. "My cock's been swollen since we met. I'm at the end of my rope on how to get you to see me as anything but an asshole."

She closed her eyes and rocked against him, the soft massage of her center against him leaving him willing to do anything to get inside of her – first her body... then her heart.

A loud knock on the glass behind him caused him to turn. He kept her pinned against the wall and smiled at Vi as she gave them a 'what the fuck?' look.

Sicily's laugh caused his heart to melt as he turned back to her.

"Come to dinner with me. Nothing more if you don't want it." He moved back and she slid down the front of his body. He took her hand and rubbed it over the front of his pants as her eyes widened. "I want a night with you. A lot of nights with you, but until you're ready, I'll wait. I just know what I want. Do you?"

"Let's finish our game and we'll start with dinner. I don't know how much more we get to after that, but I'll go another date with you." She turned and walked to pick up her racket as he growled softly. The day was turning out good, but he wanted it to be better.

Had the damn room been four solid walls, there would have been no stopping him. Stripping her down and making love to her up against one of the walls of his gym would be a fantasy come true.

He needed to talk to her about Martin, and playing an aggressive sport during the conversation seemed a better idea than busting up their date with the drama.

"Hey... I wanted to come see you last night, but when you didn't respond to my text, I figured it was better to just lay off."

She glanced around and nodded toward his hands. "Serve the ball. I was a little overwhelmed by your willingness to be so open. You don't seem like an open kinda guy."

"I'm not usually." He tossed the ball up and hit it, starting the game back up. "I want to work on becoming more than friends, so openness is part of the deal, right?"

"Yes. I'm going to work on it, too. Why did you want to come over last night? Got a new luffa you wanted to try out?" She laughed as she hit the ball against a side corner.

He rebounded after it, barely reaching it in time as he grumbled. "Tease."

He turned to catch the beautiful expression on her face. His heart fluttered and he knew he was lost. She better fall in love with him or he might have to pick up and start life again, somewhere else. Getting rejected by her and having to hang out in their friend group for the next thousand years wasn't going to fly. Seeing her with another guy certainly wasn't going to work. He'd fuck a dude up in a heartbeat for touching his girl. He should just inform her that she was stuck whether she liked it or not.

Too much. Slow your roll.

"I actually wanted to come by because I had an interesting conversation with Martin." He turned to his left and backhanded the ball.

"You went by the bakery?" She hit it back and jogged to stand next to him. The soft bounce of her breasts caused his cock to twitch again.

"Yeah. I brought you flowers and wanted to apologize for whatever you thought I meant to do at the station. I was only there to support you." He shrugged, trying to ignore the sweet smell of her perfume or soap as it wafted by him every so often.

"Flowers?" She smiled and hit the ball harder as if the idea of flowers pissed her off.

"Yeah. He told me that Judy is his grandmother." Drake hit the ball and stopped short as Sicily turned to him, her mouth dropping open. The ball popped her in the back of her shoulder and she flinched, reaching for it and letting out a yelp.

"Oh, baby. Shit." He moved toward her and forced her to turn as she growled about his timing being crappy. A smile lifted his lips as he tugged the top of her shirt down a little. "That's gonna leave a bruise."

She pulled from him and turned. "Like Judy across the street? Margaret's daughter?"

"Yeah. Exactly. Margaret's his aunt."

"What? That's fucked up." She sighed and pressed her hand to her head. "I've left him to run the shop a million times in the last few weeks. He could be burning the place down as we speak."

Her words caused Drake to pause. "Wait a minute. Paul said your sweater was in Judy's during the fire, right?"

"Paul's the big white cop?"

"Yeah. What if..." Drake pressed his finger to his lips as he turned and scanned the gym, his mind pulling two and two together. "Fuck. What if the boy dropped your sweater in there, and then set fire to the place."

"Why would he want it to burn down?" Sicily moved up to him and crossed her arms. The movement only accentuated her cleavage, causing his cock to twitch yet again.

"Stop looking so fucking sexy. I can't think." He ran his hands through his wet hair and turned, pacing up and down the court as several reasons dawned on him. "Maybe he hates them or maybe he's tired of seeing his grandmother there."

"No. That's silly." Her voice was soft, as if she were hurting. The damn ball hit her hard. He should have warned her. He moved toward her and rubbed her shoulders as she continued to look at the ground.

"Maybe insurance money. Margaret is a greedy bitch and you've taken a lot of business from them. Maybe she wants to close the place by burning it down and pinning it on you. Seems like a viable way to do it. Get her nephew to come work for you, take something of yours after earning your trust, and then set the place on fire and pin it on you."

She glanced up and sniffled, her eyes filled with tears.

His heart broke at the sight of her upset once again.

"We'll figure it all out. I'll prosecute all of them. You hear me? You have nothing to worry about. If Margaret is playing this sick game, but we'll get her." He wiped a few of the tears that rolled over her cheeks and pulled her close.

"It's not Margaret." She sniffled again and finally wrapped her arms around him, the slight tremor rushing through her leaving him more concerned.

"The ball?"

"No. You really think I'm sexy?" she whispered as a tear drilled down her cheek.

Drake let out a sharp laugh and slid his hand up to cup her face. "Are you fucking kidding me? I've been suffering a hard-on since you got into town. I'm supposed to be laying low out here in Maine and you're making me want to scream from the rooftops how I feel."

She smiled and pushed up, brushing her lips across his. "I want to go to dinner tonight."

"Then we will." He leaned down and deepened the kiss, needing to taste her once more before letting her go. The bang on the window behind him was ignored. They could kick him out... he wasn't breaking the moment again.

CHAPTER FIFTEEN

They had agreed to catch up with each other later that evening. Sicily drove to the bakery with her windows down and the radio off, needing to think through the new information on Martin. Should it matter? Not really, but seeing that Judy's was lying in a pile of rubble, and Drake had a great theory on the kid's involvement... it did.

She parked outside the bakery and sat in the car for a minute, trying to let the odd racquetball game between her and Drake dissipate. Things were moving too fast between them, and yet from what he said, he had been trying to get her attention for months. Why he hadn't given up a while back was beyond her. He was eons out of her league anyway.

Martin walked out of the shop and flipped the sign on the front to 'closed' as she opened the door and smiled at him. He had been beyond good to her. At least she could start by giving him the benefit of the doubt.

"Hey." She closed her car door and reached up, brushing her freshly showered hair from her face.

His eyes widened a little before a large smile lifted his lips. "Hey yourself, stranger. I was almost worried this morning when you weren't here."

"Yeah. Just needed to work through a few things. The intention was to get in around ten, but it's lunchtime. Where the morning went, I have no idea."

"It's no big deal. Mr. Carrington called for you. I left a message on your desk."

"Thanks. You off to lunch?" She walked past him and opened the door, flipping the sign back to 'open'.

"Yeah. You want to come?"

"No. I need to catch up on a few things." She smiled and nodded toward the road. "Stay warm. There's a cold front coming through from what I hear."

"I love this time of the year." He walked backward until his legs bumped into his car. "I was going to take an afternoon off later this week to go spend some time with my grandmother. That okay?"

She started to question him on Judy being his grandmother, but dropped it. It wasn't the right time with him heading out and the last thing she wanted to do was sound terse to someone who had picked up her slack and had held things up in her absence.

"Of course. Go this afternoon. I got this."

"You sure? You know it's always crazy on Tuesday afternoons because of half price hour at the arcade." He nodded toward the large arcade.

"I'm sure. I need the practice for when you go to college."

"You need a few more people to help you."

"I couldn't agree more. Go find a pretty girl to date and ask her if she wants a job." Sicily laughed, leaving the idea that Martin could be nefarious behind her. There was no way.

"The pretty girl I want to take out already owns the place." He winked and turned, walking to his car. "I'll see you tomorrow morning?"

"You sure will." Sicily turned and walked into her quaint little sugar shop, letting out a sigh. The kid was too much if he thought anything would happen between them. He was seventeen, for starters, and she was in love with the owner of the town's gym.

"In love?" she asked herself and dropped her purse before reaching for an apron. Had she started to fall in love with Drake? "It's been six months of him moving around the edges of your life. How can you not be in love with him? The man's a god."

"Are you talking about me when I'm not around?" Michael moved to the front counter as she let out a yelp.

"Oh, Michael. You scared the hell out of me. Were you locked in here?"

He moved to the door and reached up, tugging down the small bell that hung over the door. "Nope. Walked in right behind you, though. The bell must be busted. Need to get you a new one."

"Yes, so I don't have a heart attack." She turned and picked up her calendar and order forms before turning her attention toward him. Forgetting all about her monologue was the best plan of attack. Hopefully Michael wouldn't bring it up either.

No such luck.

The afternoon had been far too busy and not only had she needed Martin to help, but could have used three more sets of hands. Michael hadn't stayed for more than a few minutes, his visit only a quick one to add details to the event coming up. He had been complimentary in his thoughts on Drake and Sicily's feelings, but in a friendly manner, he had laid down a stark warning. If she had a chance to dig into the man's past before making a serious decision, she should do it.

"How the hell do you do that?" she muttered in the quiet confines of her car on the way home that afternoon. "Drake, can you give me your yearbooks and fill out this character questionnaire? Mind if I do a background check on you and interview your dying mother?"

She pulled up into the driveway at the house and parked, turning the car off and getting out as the wind picked up. The cold front was almost there and felt great.

How long had she been waiting for the first proper cold front so she could bundle up and hid behind a wall of sweaters? No one could blame a person for looking heavy if they had on ten layers of clothing. Winter was good like that.

Sicily walked to the door, turning at the sound of a motorcycle moving down the street. Her heart fluttered in her chest as she paused and waited for him to turn into the driveway. He parked and pulled off his helmet, his black bomber jacket fitting him tightly as it hugged his slim waist over his stone-washed jeans.

"Got flour on your nose and sugar on your lips?" He winked and walked toward her, slipping the helmet under his arm.

"No, thankfully. I try not to be nearly the mess I was when I first started. Besides, you don't like sugar, so I'm thinking if I was hoping for a goodnight kiss after our date, I'd be out of luck."

He jogged up the stairs and stopped in front of her. "I avoid it because it's addictive, but you're going to force that to change, aren't you?"

"Yes. Who else is going to taste my sticky buns to make sure they come out right?" She winked as he chuckled, the blush covering his cheeks almost as adorable as the messy state of his hair. "You're early and I'm not ready."

"I know. I just got done and didn't want to sit around the house. I got a call from my brother and my mother's not doing well. She's been on hospice for a few days and it's looking grim." He nodded toward the door and shivered. "Cold front's here. Open the door, pretty girl."

She laughed and turned, opening the door and moving into the dark house. It was chilly inside and empty from what she could tell. "Guess we're the first ones here."

His cologne smelled divine. She worked to ignore the building nervousness combined with excitement that threatened to rage within her. Going out to lunch wasn't the same as going on an official date with Drake.

The night left the possibility open to something more than food and an awkward goodbye. She wanted to see his place and snuggle up next to him, even if she wasn't entirely sure sleeping with him would be the right result. There were so many things about her own body that she wasn't ready to share. Being with him would feel so damn good, but to be bare before him was almost too much to consider. If left her with an odd sense of flight or fight, and running would soon be the result.

"Get ready and let's go. I'm starving." He moved to the couch and sat down before turning on sports center.

"Alright. Shouldn't be but a few minutes. You want me to drive since it's getting so cold?"

"I'm good driving if you don't mind snuggling up to me. The cold front is going to hit around ten tonight and it's five, so we should be good to be back from dinner and sweaty by the time ten hits."

Sicily stood there for a minute, her jaw dropping at his openness. "I'm uh... I'm not sure..."

"I'm playing, baby. Go get dressed. Whatever happens tonight is great with me. I'm a little moody thanks to D's call over mom, but being with you is making me feel better already."

"Okay." She smiled and turned, dropping her bags and walking to the bedroom as excitement sparked in her belly. Whether they stayed the rest of the night together or not, one thing was sure. Dinner would be great and the ride there and back would be blissful. Now to find something feminine that didn't leave her feeling like a popsicle due to the shifting weather.

She landed on a white sweater and black jeans with a large red belt and red heels. Her jacket wasn't in the closet, but Lisa had a really cool leather bomber that looked a lot like Drake’s. Sicily slipped it on, knowing that Lisa wouldn't care a bit over her borrowing it. She walked out as Drake looked back and whistled.

"Damn... finest woman in Bar Harbor." He stood and slipped his hands in his pockets as his eyes raked across her.

"Jake would beg to differ."

"Yeah, well he's a coach and I'm a gym rat. I could take him in a brawl over it." He winked as she laughed.

"Let's go try that new Italian place by the bay, where all of those restaurants are."

"Yeah. It's Gio's. I love it actually. I indulge on occasion." He opened the door. "It's not new, just relocated from the other side of town. The owner reminds me of my Uncle Vinny, mom's oldest brother. Good family. Great food."

"Good. Let's go support them and fill our bellies then."

"Not too much food." He lifted his eyebrow and she scoffed, ready to throw something back at his insinuation to her being chunky. "I don't want you lethargic when I start putting the moves on you."

"Pig." She laughed and swatted at him.

"Hog, baby. The bike's called a hog."

"I wasn't talking about the bike."

"Oh, I know. I know too well." He got on and offered her a hand, the look in his eyes leaving her no question over his feelings. Now to fully figure out hers.

CHAPTER SIXTEEN

Drake tried to focus on the road as they drove to Gio's, but Sicily's lithe little arms around his waist and the soft brush of her fingers over is legs a few times almost unraveled him. By the time they got there, he was sporting a less than comfortable attention grabber.

He turned and adjusted himself, grateful for her not throwing a comment his way. She knew he was interested. Now it was time to show her a little about himself and see if she could reciprocate the feeling.

Gio met them at the door, the owner having been the hostess of the restaurant since Drake found the little place a few years back.

"Mr. DeMarco. So nice to see you, and you have a lady friend? What's the world coming to?"

Sicily chuckled beside him and Drake glanced at her. "Don't laugh at him. It only encourages the old man."

"You're not getting any younger either, mister." The large Italian man with more white than grey hair moved in and shook Drake's hand before pulling him into a tight hug. "How have you been?"

"Good, Gio. This is my friend, Sicily. She's the new baker on the square."

"No? You own Sweet Treats?" Gio moved toward Sicily and pulled her into a tight side-hug.

"Yes, sir. I do."

"You're far too thin to be a baker, woman. Don't you know that we as chefs sign an unwritten set of rules, and the first is to remain chunky for our calling?" He rubbed her shoulder and released her as she beamed.

The gym had taken a few pounds off of her, but her routine with Vi had toned her up more than anything. Seeing her experience the fruits of her labor was going to be a good start to the night.

"Let's get you two a table near the window." Gio moved in front of them, holding two menus as Drake reached out, pressing softly against her lower back. Any reason to touch her was a good one.

They stopped at the table and he helped her out of her jacket before working on his. Gio took the jackets and Drake sat down and picked up the wine menu. "Red or white?"

"Whatever you think. What are we eating? We could pair it up."

"I think red goes with most tomato dishes, unless you're wanting chicken or fish."

"You've eaten here before. What do you recommend?" She brushed her long dark hair behind her shoulder, and Drake couldn't help but stifle a groan. She was by far the most beautiful, real, wholesome woman he had been around in years. Why couldn't they have started dating months back?

Oh yeah... she wouldn't let you within ten feet of her.

"I'm down with sharing the Italian Sampler. It's a great two or three bite taste of the best items on the menu." He paused as the waiter walked up.

"Evening, folks. I'm Jon. I'll be your server. Might I suggest a lovely red wine to go with something from our pasta menu tonight?"

"You sure can." Drake glanced at Sicily as she nodded, the smile on her face sweet and sexy at the same time.

"Are you ready to order or need a minute?" the young guy asked.

"What would you suggest?" Drake asked and sat back, tugging his napkin into his lap.

"The Italian Sampler is great for sharing. That and a bottle of merlot would be a fantastic start to your night." The waiter poured water in their empty glasses and smiled.

"We'll do that. Sounds great." Sicily glanced over at Drake and winked.

The server left and Drake dove into the meat of the conversation, or at least where he needed it to go. Better to get everything on the table and see where things landed.

"I know this is sudden, and I completely understand if you have to say no, but I'm leaving for Chicago on Friday afternoon to see my mother before she passes." He picked up his water glass as his hand shook slightly. Her rejection was one thing if it were to come, but his mother's condition was something much bigger. The worry and fear over it had yet to manifest, but it would soon.

"I'll go with you." Sicily reached across the table before stopping short. "I mean, if you want me to. Not that you were going to ask, I just thought..."

He lifted his hand to stop her. "That's exactly what I was going to ask. I don't want to go by myself and I feel like us getting away for a few days would help me explain a little better who I am and what I've been through."

"I would like that." She glanced down at her teeth brushed across her thick bottom lip. "I'm not sure what to do about the shop, though. Martin has been working a lot lately and leaving it for a few hours is totally different than leaving it with him for the weekend. He's just a kid."

"Yeah. I was thinking we could see if Vi and Jasmine might be able to fill in, or Kari and Jake? Lisa maybe?"

"We can do that. I'll limit the hours and get them to fill in for the times we are open." Sicily smiled up at the waiter as he delivered salads and wine.

Drake waited until he was gone to pick up the conversation again. "We fly out on Friday at three. I can pick you up and we'll just go to the airport together. My brother, Demetri, and his associate will pick us up."

"Associate? Sounds important." Sicily lifted the glass to her lips, her eyes moving across his face as he watched her.

"Have I told you how beautiful you look? I haven't wanted to sit across from a table from a woman in a long time. You leave me with absolutely no choice in the matter."

She smiled and glanced down as her cheeks colored pink. "Thanks."

"So you'll come with me, for sure?"

"Yes. I'll get my ticket tonight. We can go back to the house after this and hang out with Jake, Kari, and Lisa. We'll get online and make sure I get a seat near yours." She reached for the bread before deciding against it. Her actions were almost jerky, as if someone had popped her hand from the basket.

Drake moved it toward him and lightly buttered a piece before extending it to her, giving her no choice in the matter. He worked on his and glanced up, loving the curious way she watched him. "D got the tickets. No need to buy anything. Just come with me."

"Are you sure you're okay with me being there? You need to spend time with your mom."

"I'll only have a few minutes to see her. D's working out the cameras and such so we can slip in and out without being seen." Drake sat back and took a bite of his bread. "A few minutes is all I need to say thank you and goodbye."

"Thank you?" Sicily lifted her eyebrow as she started to eat her salad. Her dainty movements were adorning. His heart swelled in anticipation of getting to know her more.

"Yeah. She loved me with this openness that I've yet to experience since. It was the type of love you could only hope for. The kind that said, 'I know you're not perfect, but it's all right. You're mine and that's enough.'" He shrugged as hard emotion pulled at him. He didn't mind being open and raw in front of her, but not in the middle of a crowded restaurant.

"I love that. My mom was the same way. My brother was a hellion in school, always getting in gang fights or sleeping with some poor unsuspecting chick in his bedroom in the house. I can't imagine raising a boy like him." Sicily laughed and took another bite of her salad. "But... my mom was forever reminding him how much she loved him. How much she loved all of us."

The pretty girl across the table from him teared up and he reached over, brushing his fingers down her arm.

"I'm sorry," she whispered.

"No. Don't be. We share this pain and it seems like our moms had a lot in common. This weekend I'll tell you anything you want to know. Let's eat dinner and then we'll go to the house and spend time with our friends. Remind me and I'll call the girls at the gym to see if they are free to help us when we leave."

"Okay. I'd like that." She smiled as the food arrived and was laid before them.

"This is enough to feed ten people." Drake chuckled and glanced up as Gio stopped by, the old man squeezing his shoulder tightly.

"Good thing you're a big boy. Your little woman over there is going to be of no help. Call for me if you need another fork to assist you." The older man laughed and walked off. "Enjoy."

Sicily blushed again.

Drake stopped, watching her as she fixed a plate and extended it to him.

She paused as her eyes widened a little. "What? Did I do something?"

Drake took the plate and set it down as he licked at his lips. "No. I've just been waiting for this moment for six months. Let me take it in."

"You're ridiculous. You're way out of my league, Drake. I should be the one needing a minute." She fixed her own plate and sat back.

"You're right. I am way out of your league, but don't tell anyone that the princess has decided to date a frog." He winked.

"As long as you're sure you become a prince... I'm good."

"Does this mean I get a kiss?" He lifted his eyebrow and chuckled as she shook her head.

"Typical frog... always looking for a kiss."

CHAPTER SEVENTEEN

They finished dinner and needed a doggie back, the small container holding more food than they ate between the two of them. Sicily walked beside Drake to the front of the restaurant and leaned into the hug with Gio, the man quickly finding his way to her heart.

Good food, great atmosphere, and how many times had he called her little or insinuated that she was too tiny to be a chef? She was sold.

"Delicious." Drake opened the door and smiled as she moved past him. His dark hair and eyes left her feeling feverish. Were they really going to go hang out with their friends?

"I agree. Great choice." Sicily stopped by the nearest trashcan and dropped the food into it as Drake let out a growl.

"What was that for? Jake and Kari would have torn that up." He moved up beside her and touched the trashcan with a look on his face that would be fitting for burying a family pet.

Sicily laughed and slid her hand into his. "I agree, but we're not going to my house."

"Oh? We're not? Where do you want to go?" He moved them toward the bike and handed her the helmet on the back. "To a movie, or the mall?"

"To your house." She slipped on the helmet and laughed as he stood there, staring at her with his mouth agape. "Come on before I change my mind."

"Hell yes." He got on the bike and started it, rubbing at her arms as they wrapped around him.

She leaned in and snuggled up to the back of him the best she could.

Their relationship wasn't new, but developing quickly. He had been trying since the night they met, Drake having come to help Jake and Kari paint the shop with her and Lisa. A smile brushed by her mouth and she turned to watch the large homes whiz past them as they drove back toward the edge of town. Sicily realized she didn't have the slightest clue where Drake lived.

The lights of the bay disappeared behind her and the darkness of the wooded area of Bar Harbor rose up ahead of them, something about it screaming serenity. The cold front moved in just before they pulled up to a small log cabin, the house quaint, but fitting for the middle of the woods.

Sicily shivered and climbed off the bike before pulling off her helmet. "Do you have a fireplace?"

"Of course I do." He winked at her. "Let's get you inside and I'll grab some wood from out back and get us warmed up."

"Sounds good." She walked toward the house beside him.

Drake reached back and took her hand, lifting it to his lips and kissing her knuckles softly. "You know we can just drink a cup of something warm and talk. I don't expect anything from you."

She smiled, grateful that he was the type of man to make sure she knew that. "I know. I just want to be with you. Whatever that means is okay."

He smiled just before sadness raced across his face. "Me too."

She started to ask what was wrong, but decided to leave it be. He would talk about whatever was raging inside of him if she just offered a comfortable place for him to land.

The inside of the house was masculine; the perfect bachelor pad. Dark woods and the smell of pine filled the place. The thick, cream-colored rugs were made of some type of animal fur and the guns on the wall gave her a whole new understanding of Drake. He was a hunter. A man's man. Why was she not surprised by that?

He moved into the house, turning on lights as she stopped by the gun cabinet and ran her fingers over the glass. "My father had a case just like this. You hunt?"

"I do. On occasion." He moved toward her and brushed his fingers over her shoulders. "Do you?"

"I haven't before, but I'd like to go with you, maybe?" She leaned back and he wrapped his arms around the top of her shoulders, bending over and pressing a kiss to the side of her neck.

"I'll take you anywhere. Anytime." He kissed her again before releasing her.

"There's a kettle on the stove. You wanna fill it up with water and start it? I'll grab some wood for us."

"Yeah. You bet." Sicily moved into the tiny kitchen, the house nothing more than three rooms from what she could tell. The living room was the largest room in the house and a small two person table sat just beside the kitchen. The darkened room behind her had to be his bedroom.

He walked out of the house and she turned, walking into the darkness and breathing in deeply. The scent of his cologne and body wash rolled over her, leaving her wanting more than a cup of something warm. She wanted him, but pushing anything didn't seem her part to play, or maybe it was.

She walked back out and got busy on the water kettle as he toted an armful of wood into the house. She moved to the front door, closing it and walking to stand beside him as he loaded the hearth with it.

"Will we get to see any of your brothers and sisters this weekend, or were you really serious about everyone thinking you're dead?" She took a seat on the couch near him and pulled her legs up under her.

Drake worked on the fire as he spoke to her. "Only D, Izzy, and my mother know I'm alive. Everyone else thinks I died, which is for the better."

"Because your father is a notorious mobster?"

He glanced around and gave her a tight smile. "That's the least of it. He's a bastard and a cold-blooded killer. He wants what's his and if anyone touches it or takes it... he'll kill them."

"Who is Izzy?"

"She's my sister, but she doesn't know that. She thinks I'm just D's brother who Joe hates. No one knows that I'm Joe's son but D, Joe, my mom, and me." He shrugged.

"Oh. Izzy is Joe's kid?"

"Yeah, one of many. She's his enforcer. In the mafia world, that's the one who goes out and murders on cue."

Sicily swallowed before pulling her legs in tighter. "Um... that sounds fucking scary. Are we going to be safe?"

He chuckled and stood, placing the gate back in front of the fire as the kettle let out a whistle. Sicily started to move, but he held up his hand.

"I'll get it." He moved to the kitchen before answering her. "We're safe. Izzy wouldn't hurt me, and D's there if nothing else."

"Your brother seems like a good guy, of sorts." She was reaching, but wanted to try to understand without judging too much. She didn't know their world and honestly didn't want to.

"He is." Drake turned around. "You want something warm to drink?"

"Not right now. Come here and talk to me." She patted the couch beside her.

He moved over and sat down, reaching for her and tugging her closer to him. "We don't need D or Izzy to protect us. I was a part of that world for twelve years before I got out. I know how to defend myself and anyone else I love from just about anything."

Sicily turned and looked up at him as the fire crackled in front of them. The shadows that played along his face left her with worry. He looked like a sexy villain that could tear a city down if needed.

What he had done in his past was something she wanted to know more about, but there had to be boundaries around it. His past was just that – the past. It couldn't affect how she saw him now. He wasn't that man anymore and from what she could see, he had given up everything to be a new man, with a new life.

He slid his fingers along her face before leaning down and brushing his lips by hers. "You look so good on this couch next to me. In this place with me."

"You look so good all the damn time." She smiled and turned, pulling him in closer as she shifted and tugged him on top of her. The soft brush of his lips was calming, but the raging need to belong to him forced her to push the moment a little.

Her tongue pressed against his lips and he groaned before opening his mouth and sucking it in deeply. Sicily tightened her grip on him and opened her legs, making room for him to snuggle in intimately. Drake ground against her, the thick press of his arousal causing her insides to melt.

"Fuck, I want you." He licked at her mouth before breaking the kiss. "You smell so good, baby."

"I want you, too." Sicily arched her back and reached up, brushing her fingers along his face as he licked at his lips.

Her phone buzzed in her purse, but she ignored it. Whatever it was... it could wait.

"Stay with me tonight. Let me make love to you." He tucked his face against the side of her neck and ran his hands over her hips, his fingers pressing into the soft skin.

"As long as you promise me it's not a one night stand. We're around each other too much to..."

Drake glanced up and cut her off. "Hush. I'm not interested in anything short-term. You're the first woman I've wanted in my life in as long as I can remember. I want to make love to you every night, but I won't ask for that promise until you see my life fully."

"I *have* seen your life, Drake." Sicily ran her fingers down his face before cupping his cheek and leaning up, brushing her lips by his. The desire to slip into a long night of fucking with the handsome man above her jolted through her system and she whimpered. "No more talking."

"Yeah, I agree, lover." He got up and extended his hand. "Let's go to my bedroom where we can spread you out properly."

The nefarious look on his handsome face caused her stomach to tighten. She chuckled and stood as her phone rang.

Worry grabbed her and held her in place as he worked to tug her toward the darkened room just beyond the kitchen.

"Let me get that. Something's up. I can tell by it buzzing so much." She let out a sigh and picked up her purse, pulling the phone out as it began to ring again.

Lisa.

"Hey, what's up?" Sicily answered with more angst than she wanted.

"Fuck, Sis. Where are you?"

"With Drake. What's the matter?" Sicily dropped Drake's hand and moved toward the door as the reception on the phone caused it to crackle a little.

"You need to get home."

"Is something wrong? What happened? Is Kari okay?"

"Yes. The fucking cops are in the living room. They say they have a warrant for your arrest."

"My arrest?" Sicily reached out and pressed her hand to the wall beside her as her knees went weak. Drake's arms wrapped around her as she tried to make sense of the conversation.

"Yes. For the fire at Judy's. I know it's shit, but you have to get here... now."

"It's the middle of the night." Sicily turned to look up at Drake as tears burned her eyes.

"They don't care. Get here, okay? Be careful and we'll work through all of this like we always do... together."

Sicily nodded and hung up the phone as Drake grabbed her shoulders.

"What the hell was that?" His face was a mask of carefully contained anger.

"The cops are at the house. They're there to arrest me for the fire at Judy's. I didn't do it. I didn't do anything wrong."

CHAPTER EIGHTEEN

The drive back to town almost killed him, the situation before his girl a serious one. The last thing he wanted to do was stand in front of the cops and watch them take her on false charges, but that's exactly what they did. Drake crossed his arms over his chest, the argument doing nothing but upsetting the officers and Drake more. Jake had tried to get involved, but they shut him down, too.

There was nothing more he could do in the moment and he decided to back off when tears dripped onto Sicily's pretty face and she asked him to stop. Her whisper tore through him and he couldn't help but feel the desire to burn down the whole fucking city.

He waited until the cop car left to get onto his phone. His brother D wouldn't be thrilled about the late night call, but he didn't give a shit.

"Drake. What's up, man? Wrong phone."

"Fuck the phone. My girl's been set up with some shit and I need your intel."

"Anything. What do you want from us?"

"Edward still working for you?"

"Yes. You want me to have him hack into the police department there and clear her on misleading evidence or what?"

"No. I need the cameras from around the city. I think I know who did this shit, but the kid involved has an Aunt who sleeps with the fucking Mayor. If the kid is on those videos as our criminal, then that will solve the problem."

"And open a whole new bucket of worms for you to deal with. It would implicate the lady and the mayor."

"Good. Fucking do it. Send me the videos now if Ed is available to dick with it."

"You sure you want this exposure? It's dangerous for you." D's voice held a tight warning.

"Do it. Now." Drake didn't care about anything but saving Sicily at the moment.

"I'll get him right this minute. What else?"

"Nothing. I'm going to beat this kid's ass for fucking with Sicily." Drake glanced over his shoulder as he stood in the yard. Jake approached him, nodding as if asking if he could come closer. "I gotta go, man. Just do that and we'll be good. See you Friday."

Drake dropped the call and slipped his phone into his pocket before turning around. "Fuck."

"This is horrible, man. We know she didn't do that shit, but how to we prove that to the cops? Paul wouldn't even look at me tonight. He knows something's wrong with the situation."

"It's fucking Margaret. You know that bitch has her fingers in all the right holes." Drake growled and ran his hands through his hair. "I have a friend pulling the cameras. I'm going to go up there tonight. No way is my girl spending the night in a cell. That's not happening."

"I'll go with you."

"No. I got this, but thanks, my man. You might need to hold me back from kicking that kid, Martin's ass. The boy is only seventeen and I don't need it on my record that I whooped some kid's ass."

"He needs his ass whooped." Jake shook his head. "He's been a huge pain this year at the high school from what their head coach was telling me."

"How so?"

"Entitlement. He thinks he should have the starting spot though he's not earned it. You know guys like him who think they deserve something and don't work to earn it or wait to get it, but simply take it."

Drake growled again and walked to his bike. "I'll call you later. Just keep Lisa and Kari calm. Lisa's ready to sue the whole damn police force."

"As she should." Jake shook his head. "It's sad what greed can do."

"Don't I know it? I used to live my life with greed as the main reason for doing everything."

"Where'd that getcha?" Jake turned and walked backwards, sadness on his face.

"Here... living as a ghost until Sicily showed up. She's my chance at a new life. I can feel it to the deepest part of my soul."

"Then go get her. Just be careful."

Drake nodded and started the bike, pulling out and not caring about anything but getting Sicily cleared.

It was just after midnight when the information finally made it to his phone from D. Edward was wicked fast, but waiting more than a few minutes left Drake a nervous ball of angst.

He paced in the lobby of the station, the pretty cop who sat up front reminding him that he shouldn't be there for the millionth time. In the sleepy city of Bar Harbor the police station probably hadn't been open past working hours for years.

Tonight it was buzzing with activity. Drake tried hard not to think about how scared his girl was. Where was she? Were they questioning her again? What did they have other than the fucking sweater?

The DNA testing had to have come back that the sweater was hers, but it wasn't enough and yet... here they sat.

Fucking Margaret.

Her actions better have been greed for insurance money, like he first thought, and not revenge. Sicily not only had moved into the middle of the square and taken half of her business, but if Martin told the saucy bitch about Sicily and Drake... she would be pissed over that as well. How many times had Margaret hit on him at the gym?

"Too many," he muttered and stood as his phone pulled up the images from Edward.

Three different short clips that showed the blond, lanky kid who sold Sicily a bag of lies going into the shop with a sweater over his arm and a bag on his back. The explosion happened a few minutes after he walked out.

I'm going to kill him.

The little fucker walked across the street and opened Sicily's shop, walking in like nothing ever happened. Why hadn't the videos been shown to the cops? Because Margaret was sleeping with the mayor. D was right... this was going to get ugly before it got cleared up.

Drake didn't give two shits. The whole world could crumble before him before he let anything happen to Sicily. He stood and walked to the counter as the female cop looked up, exasperation sitting on her face.

"Mr. DeMarco, you really should go home. Nothing is going to change tonight."

"Yes, it is. Get Paul up here."

"He's not willing to see you just yet. They are reviewing additional..."

Drake turned and walked toward the hall, yelling, "Paul. Get your ass out here."

"Mr. DeMarco. We'll arrest you if you don't..." The girl moved toward him and Drake turned, pinning her with a stare that made her think twice about coming close to him.

Paul yelled from down the hall, his voice laced with worry and exhaustion. "Drake. Come on back, man. I have ten minutes before I leave. You can have it."

Drake didn't pay attention to the girl again, but walked toward the detective who had to play cop, coffee maker, and receptionist due to them being short staffed most days of the week.

"She didn't do this," Drake barked as they walked down the hall.

"As a cop I'll tell you that I can't discuss this with you." Paul turned on the light in a small room and held the door for him. "As your friend, I'll tell you to stop representing girls you're in love with."

Drake walked in and took a seat before sliding his phone across the table. "As Miss Moretti's legal counsel, I'll tell you that you guys have something much worse on your hands than the cake wars you think you're in the middle of."

Paul glanced down at the phone. "What's this?"

"Where are the camera clips from the early morning when Judy's was set on fire, Paul?"

"The county told us they were destroyed because of the electrical explosion of the fire."

"They fucking lied. Check it out." Drake nodded toward the phone as Paul let out a long breath and fell into a seat.

Drake would bet his life on the fact that Paul wasn't involved in whatever cover up Margaret was working on. The guy seemed too legit and good-hearted to be, but stranger things had happened.

Paul watched the videos, his complexion paling significantly with each one. "Son of a bitch."

"Let her go or I'll press charges against the police station for extortion."

Paul glanced up. "You wouldn't do that. I had no part in this."

"That's my woman you have locked up back there. I know her and she's scared and probably mentally diving into a deep hole. I would wreck every barrier I had to in order to get to her." Drake narrowed his eyes and squeezed his hands into tight fists as the room seemed to grow darker around him. There wasn't anything he wouldn't do for Sicily.

"Send these to me and post bail for her. I'll have you refunded tomorrow when we go live with the truth. I didn't know." Paul stood and walked to the door. "Wait out front and I'll release her to you."

"Fine." Drake stood and walked to the front as he worked to e-mail the files to Paul. He looked up at the officer and gave her a credit card. "Post bail for her and bring her to me."

The officer nodded and stood up. She disappeared into the back for a minute and returned with a file in her hands. She was swiping Drake's card as Paul rounded the corner with Sicily next to him. The pretty girl let out a soft cry and ran to Drake as he moved toward her.

Wrapping his arms around her, he picked her up and pressed his face against the crook of her neck. "It's okay, baby. I'm here. Nothing's gonna happen to you now."

CHAPTER NINETEEN

Drake took her home the night before, but left shortly after. Some part of her wanted to invite him to stay the night, but she couldn't. She needed to cry out her fear and humiliation alone. That the police would really think her capable of doing something so heinous weighed heavily on her.

She woke the next morning, still torn over what to do about Martin. He had been the one to tear her name down and throw her under the bus. He didn't need to go into baking, but acting. The little shit had her completely fooled.

Drake told her to call when she woke up, but she couldn't stand the thought of sounding so pathetic on the phone to him. She would call later when she got her bearings. First thing was first... she needed to fire Martin and give him a piece of her mind.

The cops should have picked him up already, but if his aunt Margaret was as powerful as Drake said she was, then chances of him even knowing about being caught were slim. It was almost a family affair at that point. The only damage done had been to Judy's, so it would be up to Margaret to press charges, which she would have to do if she wanted the insurance funds.

"Hey," Lisa mumbled as she looked up from the kitchen table.

Sicily walked in and made her way to the coffee pot. "Hey. Kari already gone?"

"Yeah. She and Jake wanted to get their day started. She said to tell you she's thinking about you." Lisa got up and walked over, pulling Sicily into a tight hug as she turned. "You okay?"

Sicily relaxed against her closest friend. "Yeah. Just still a little shaken by all of it. I wouldn't be out of that creepy ass cell if Drake hadn't have pulled a few strings. Thank God for him."

"How did he get ahold of those videos? Jake said they were ruined from the explosion."

"The county lied, I guess." Sicily shrugged. "No clue how he got them, and I don't care. I'm just grateful."

"You still going out of town with him this weekend?" Lisa moved back and brushed her hand down the back of Sicily's hair.

"I don't think so. I want to, but I really think I need to be at the shop. Who knows where all of this shit is going?" Sicily turned and fixed a to-go mug of coffee.

"We'll be here to deal with all this shit. You need to go. It's obvious that he cares deeply for you. Don't waste the chance to spend some time with him." Lisa gave her a knowing look.

"I'll think about it." Sicily forced a tight smile and picked up her keys.

Going with Drake to Chicago would be a great way to look into his life a little and make sure she belonged there. Her hormones and heart were sold on the idea, but the fact that he was capable of pulling so many strings meant he was *still* powerful. The life might be in the past, but like a well-worn picture book, he had access to bring it out and breathe life into it at any time.

If they got together and things didn't work... would he let her live her life outside of him or would he force her to stay close? He seemed like the controlling type. Where she was grateful for his ability to help her, and quite taken with him, her brother was right... he was dangerous.

"In more ways than one." She pulled up to the bakery and got out quickly. Martin's truck was there, which meant the little shit wasn't in jail. "Surprise, surprise."

She walked into the shop as a bell jingled above her. Turning to look up at it, the sound of his voice behind her caused her to jump.

"Mr. Carrington dropped that off this morning."

"Oh." She turned and pinned him with a stare. "We need to talk."

"You bet." A beeper went off in the back room and he nodded. "Let me grab that and I'll come right back out. It's a fresh batch of cinnamon rolls. I think I got them right, finally. I swear I thought I was going to have to bake them every night this week at home to get them to be more like yours."

She put her purse up as he disappeared into the back room. Sadness sat on her at the conversation to come. The kid wasn't nefarious from what she could tell. He had to simply be a tool to those that were though. He thought he would get away with it. Or at least she prayed that was the case. To have him be a bad guy would temporarily shatter her faith in humanity.

Sicily worked to get the register ready as sickness rolled through her. She didn't like confrontations, but the conversation had to come from her. Everyone had stepped up to help her run the shop over the next few days so she could get away with Drake, but now just didn't seem like the right time.

"Okay. They look good, but they still aren't yours." Martin stopped beside her and hopped up to sit on the counter. "You look beautiful today."

"Thanks." She glanced up at him before putting some space between them. Sicily wrapped her arms around herself as tears burned her gaze. She wasn't going to cry, but the situation left her no choice. Why anyone would want to hurt her was beyond her.

"What's wrong? Did something happen? Did Mr. DeMarco hurt you? I can help, Sis." He moved toward her and she held her hand up.

"No. I spent half the night in jail last night for the fire at Judy's. I would never hurt anyone – ever. They took my fingerprints and berated me that your grandmother was in the hospital, as if my nasty attack on Margaret's bakery led her there. I've been nothing but good to your family." She let out a small sob. "I've taught you everything I know and treated you like my own family."

Martin paled visibly, his warm gaze growing wide with fear. "I didn't have a choice, Sicily. They didn't leave me a choice in the matter. They have more power than anyone in the city."

He moved toward her and she shook her head, her voice gaining strength. "No. Everyone has a choice. You made yours, so get out. If the cops don't pick you up soon, then I have no faith in anything in this shitty little dot on the map."

"Don't do this. You know I wouldn't hurt you." He moved to stand in front of her, sliding his hands over her shoulders as she tried to jerk away.

"Stop it. Get out and take your lack of options with you." She choked on another sob, pissed at herself for caring for the kid like she would a brother. He obviously didn't have enough sense in his head to care about his future. The truth almost always came out... and now his life would be forever changed because of his shitty decisions.

"No. Don't do this. I'm sorry. I can fix it." He pulled her to him, wrapping his arms around her as she jerked back to find the counter pinning her in place.

"Get your hands off of me, Martin."

"No. I love you. I'm sorry and I'll make it right. Don't pull away from me. You know we belong together. One day we'll own this beautiful little shop together and everything will be all right. I'll spend my life making it up to you." He took her face in his hands as she pushed at his stomach.

"Get off!"

The sound of Drake's bark almost caused her blood to run cold. The hate on his handsome face was shocking as he barreled into the shop and caught Martin by the back of the neck. Drake jerked the kid so hard that he flew into a group of tables and chairs and landed with a sickening crunch.

"You sorry motherfucker. Thinking you were going to fuck my girl's name up and get away with it?" Drake turned and went after Martin as he tried to stand.

"Drake. No. Leave him alone. The cops can deal with him. You don't need to."

Drake picked the kid up and punched him in the face three times in quick succession before Sicily could get to him. The boy's head lolled to the side as he passed out.

Sicily grabbed Drake's arm as he lifted it to punch him again, the handsome man she'd given her heart to nowhere to be found.

The guy in front of her had blood on his hands and vengeance in his gaze.

"Stop it!" Sicily screamed at him as she tugged his arm back.

"He has to pay for what the fuck he did. This isn't a simple situation, Sicily. He fucked us over."

"He fucked *me* over. I'm good with the cops having at him. Put him down and get out. You're going to kill him."

"He deserves to feel the pain of what he did. Move back." Drake turned his hard gaze onto her and she saw the killer he used to be. A tremor ran through her as she slapped him in the face hard.

He dropped the boy and turned to face her.

"Get out. Now. You're no better than you used to be. You're not a new man, but the same man you've always been."

Her words caused him to visibly flinch, but brought realization to his gaze. He nodded once and walked to the door as his shoulders slumped.

"Drake. I didn't mean that. Please. I just don't want..."

He cut her off, lifting his hand as he scoffed. "No, it's good. You're right. It was a monster who fell in love with you. Who dropped everything and risked his safety to call in favors to save you. Who showed up today to remind you that you're loved and cherished?"

Sicily glanced toward the door to see roses scattered everywhere. Her stomach fell as she walked toward him.

Martin groaned on the floor next to her and she realized she needed to call the police or an ambulance. Someone had to help the boy, but first Drake needed to hear her heart.

"I'm sorry."

"Yep. Me too. All this time you've been so fucking concerned with me judging you and yet you're the only one in the judgment seat."

"I would never judge you. Ever."

"You already have, baby. Good luck with this stuff. I'll be around if you need legal assistance." He nodded and walked out, his eyes cold and words true.

She had judged him, and now he was gone.

CHAPTER TWENTY

"I'm sorry you had to deal with this, Miss. Moretti." The lead officer on her case shook his head and kept his eyes turned toward the ground.

"It's okay. I just wish Martin wouldn't have been the criminal in this." She forced a smile as Paul glanced up, the man having been a good friend to Drake during the whole process. For that, she was grateful.

"And you're sure you want this record to read that *you* put a hurting on the boy that has him going to the hospital?" The cop lifted his eyebrow and tilted his head slightly. He had to have known it was Drake who laid the wayward teen out on the ground.

"Yes. He attacked me and I acted in self-defense. I'm from the streets of New York, officer." She shrugged and moved her gaze to rest behind him as the paramedic's loaded Martin up in the ambulance. "He's going to be okay, right?"

"Yeah. Just standard procedure." Paul turned and let out a long sigh. "Alright, well, we'll get your name cleared at the station, and if anything pops up from this, I'll let you know. I would have assumed his Aunt Margaret was going to strike back, but seeing that she's the one who put the poor kid up to burning down her bakery... I don't know. She might tuck tail and run."

"I have no idea how I got wrapped up in all of this. I've been so kind to Margaret and her family. Heck, I even went over to their bakery when I first got into town to see what I shouldn't offer in my own. I didn't want to be in competition with them. I was looking for a new life here. One that would be different from the back-stabbing mentality of New York."

"I understand. Small towns aren't much better than big cities, though. They have the same thing in common, you know?"

"What's that?" Sicily ran her fingers through her hair before working it into a messy bun.

"Greedy people with little to no conscience." He chuckled and tucked his pad back into his back pocket. "Alright. If you're good, I'm going to go. Nothing else to tell me, right?"

"We're good. I've said all I'm saying." She shrugged and walked him to the door.

He nodded and gave her a knowing smirk, but didn't say another word.

Shutting the door, Sicily let the first wave of her internal trauma release. A soft sob left her as tears blurred her vision.

Drake was right. She had judged him before he could ever get the chance to judge her. Was it a defense mechanism or was she really no better than everyone else who judged the people around them? The look on his face told her that it wasn't going to be easy to get back into his good graces. Did she want to?

"Yes," s+he whispered and walked to the counter, picking up a towel and wiping her eyes. She sneezed several times as white powder flew up around her. The rag had powdered sugar on it, which left her sneezing several more times.

The humor in the moment wasn't lost on her as she laughed through her tears. How had her life gotten so fucked up all of a sudden?

"I don't know, but I need to get him back." She brushed the back of her hand across her face and pulled out her phone, staring at the last text he sent.

If there were something she could say to help him understand why she'd blown up so quickly. It was fear and high emotion. *Right?*

No. After talking with her brother, Johnny, earlier in the week she had started to question Drake. It was like living on a nonstop roller coaster for the last few weeks. One minute she was willing to forgive his past, even though she didn't truly understand what he'd done or who he'd been. The next she was ready to run for the hills.

Her phone rang and she yelped, jumping as Kari's number popped up.

"Hey," Sicily mumbled into the phone.

"Are you okay? We're headed up there right now." Kari's tone was sharp and filled with fear.

"I'm okay. The cops just left." Sicily moved to the front door and glanced out, wishing like hell Drake's bike was still out front. "How did you know what happened?"

"Drake called Jake and said for us to get up here to support you."

"Of course he did." Tears filled her eyes again. How many times had he helped her in the last few weeks? Innumerable. She had stabbed him deeply and he was still helping. She didn't deserve a man like him. He was working to overcome his demons and she was kicking him back down the side of the mountain he was working to scale on his own.

"Did he hurt you?" Jake's voice surprised her.

"What? No. He was protecting me, but I told the cops it was me who whooped Martin's ass. I'll explain when you get here. Drake has been nothing but good to me. I wish I could say the same for myself." She let out a sigh and hung up.

She needed to call him. A simple apology spoken in honesty and love would start them on the path to healing. Before she could back out of calling, she hit the button and bit into her bottom lip. The call went directly to his voicemail, which was full – of course.

She called again twice more and got nothing. Nothing could be easy... nothing.

Kari and Jake showed up a few minutes later and helped fix up the bakery before splitting up for the ride home. Jake drove his truck and Kari took the keys to Sicily's car to drive her back to the house.

Sicily's stomach growled loudly as she buckled up and leaned back in her seat.

"You hungry, hun?" Kari reached out and squeezed Sicily's hand.

"I guess." She glanced at the clock, realizing that it was early afternoon. "I didn't eat breakfast and with all the drama, lunch passed me right by too."

"We were going to make sub sandwiches."

"You and Jake?" Sicily turned to watch her pretty friend.

"No. He was at work. He came by the house to grab me after Drake called him. Lisa and I were making sandwiches. She had a fit to come get you, but we figured too many people might make you a little crazy. Jake wouldn't take no for an answer on coming, so it was me and him." She shrugged and pulled her hand back into her own lap.

"A sandwich sounds good." Sadness filled up the entire space of her chest and she pressed her hands to her face to keep from crying. "I'm so angry at myself."

"Why? This isn't your fault. That fucking kid set you up, Sis."

"No. Martin is water under the bridge. I'll figure that out later. I totally judged Drake and slung a bunch of harsh accusations at him before he walked out of the bakery today. I hate myself right now. The one thing I never want done to me, and I just did it to the guy I'm falling in love with."

"You're falling in love with him?" Kari turned and stared at me.

"Yeah. Not that it matters now."

"Of course it does. You just need to call him, and explain what happened, Sicily. What went down today is a big deal. No one would have handled it well."

"You should have seen the look on his face when I attacked him." She let out a painful sigh. "I should have just taken an axe and chopped him in half. It wouldn't have hurt him as much."

"It's going to be okay. He's falling in love with you, too, you know."

"Yeah, was falling. I'm not so sure he's willing to give me a second chance." Sicily shrugged and unbuckled as they pulled up to the house. "Thanks for coming after me."

"Anytime." Kari reached out and rubbed Sicily's shoulder. "We're going to figure this out, okay? You're not alone in all of this."

"Thanks," Sicily mumbled and got out of the car as the cold wind of early winter picked up. She shivered and walked to the door as Kari leaned against the car, obviously waiting on Jake.

Kari has a great relationship. Lisa has an incredible thing with Marc, and I have nothing. Whatever was starting to form with Drake is blown to hell and back.

Sicily opened the door and didn't make it more than a step inside before Lisa was wrapping her in a tight hug.

"Oh, my God. I was scared to fucking death. What the fuck happened?" Lisa squeezed harder and Sicily relaxed into her best friend's hold, letting a soft sob go. "Oh, Sis. Come on. Let's go get you into something comfy and you can tell me all about it."

Sicily pulled back and sniffled. "Okay."

"Kari and Jake are back, too?"

"Yeah. Kari's waiting out front for Jake." She shrugged and walked down the hall in front of Lisa.

"Jake gave me a shortened version of what happened, but I want to hear it firsthand, if you're up to it."

Sicily walked into her room and tugged off her clothes and kicked off her shoes before walking to the dresser. She pulled out an old T-shirt and some sweats.

"I was set up by Margaret to make it look like I set Judy's on fire. She had Martin come work for me, take my sweater and leave it in their shop, and then start the damn fire." Sicily turned and walked to the bed, dropping down and scooting up to lay down beside Lisa.

"Insane. I thought my life was crazy having to contend with Michael Carrington and Marc, but yours is much worse. So Drake showed up and kicked the boy's ass because of all of that?"

"That, and really because Martin was physically holding me still. He was interested in something with me and I guess he thought with enough fear and force I would simply succumb to his advances." Sicily reached over and brushed Lisa's copper hair off her shoulder.

"He's like seventeen. You're twenty-three. That's... gross."

"Yes, I know that. I never gave him any inclination that I was interested, but he got it in his head that he and I were on our way to becoming something special. Drake had come by to check on me, but it was piss poor timing on Martin's part."

"How was the ass whooping? I bet Drake put a hurting on that creep."

"It was scary, actually. Drake has some dark stuff in his past. He's not really shared any of that with me, but I threw it in his face after seeing the monster he turned into with Martin." Sicily turned onto her back. "It was honestly more frightening watching Drake go nuts than dealing with anything else I've dealt with lately."

"Did you think he would hurt you?"

"No. Never." Sicily let out a sigh and glanced over at Lisa. "I thought he was going to kill Martin though. He had that look in his eye that said he wasn't going to stop beating the kid until he did permanent damage."

"What's in his past that you're worried about?"

"I don't really know. I just know he was involved in some gang-type stuff. I was going with him this weekend to Chicago and we were going to talk about it. In order to move into a real relationship together, he thinks I need to completely understand what I'm getting myself into."

"I like that." Lisa scooted closer and snuggled into Sicily's side.

"I did too, but it's irrelevant now."

"How so?"

"He left the shop after I attacked him, and his parting words were basically, 'good luck with life'."

"He was hurt, Sis. That's probably better than what we could have said."

"True, but he's not answering his phone."

"So you're not at all worried that he might hurt you?" Lisa moved up on her elbow and glanced down at Sicily.

"No. Not in the slightest. I love him, Lisa."

Lisa's lips turned up into a bright smile. "Then text him and tell him that you're going to Chicago. Act like nothing's changed. What do you have to lose?"

She was right. There was nothing else to lose where Drake was concerned. The worse thing he could tell her was that she wasn't allowed to go. Chances are he wouldn't do that.

"You're right." Sicily sat up and picked up her phone, pulling up her texts and saying a small prayer before shooting off a note.

CHAPTER TWENTY-ONE

Drake parked his bike around the back of the shop and walked languidly to the front. His thoughts assaulted him left and right. No matter how hard he tried to put the scene out of his head, he kept coming back to the same place. Sicily standing there, horrified by him. He had been too aggressive with the kid, though the little punk ass deserved every minute of it.

Sicily obviously didn't agree.

Her words were harsh, and though he knew she didn't truly mean them, he couldn't convince himself otherwise. It was good that she had seen firsthand what a monster he could be. It had been a peaceful five years, but good fortune never lasted long in his life. The mob would come calling sometime soon and he would have to return. The sins of his past owed him a life of hell. Sicily didn't need to get involved in with him.

She can do much better. I want her to.

Drake walked into the gym and nodded at Violet as she glanced up from the appointment book.

"Hey, boss. How goes... oh." Her expression changed, the joy fading to worry.

"Don't ask. Just let me know if you need me. I'm going to do some paperwork and then hit the weights." He glanced her way and walked by the desk, not waiting for her response.

The girls at the gym were like sisters to him. When he'd first hired them, each had taken a turn to try and force something to happen between the two of them, but he wouldn't have any of it.

Work and pleasure had to be separate. It was too damn hard to stay objective about someone you cared about.

After years of working together, he had them all healthy, happy, and fully functional. Now if someone would make that shit happen in *his* life.

His phone buzzed in his pocket and he ignored it. There was no one that he wanted to talk to, including Sicily. She had tried to backtrack the minute he walked toward the door, but he wasn't interested in a shallow relationship. She needed to stew in her accusations and he needed to reconsider where he was really willing to let their involvement go.

Sexually, he was all in. She was the center of his desire, her body every fucking thing he wanted beneath his. Her drive and stamina to make it in her bakery shop left him aching for more time around her, and her personality and laughter was spot on. Nothing was missing where he was concerned, but his desire wasn't enough to sustain a relationship. She had to make the call, and where losing control in any situation wasn't something he desired, he didn't have a choice in the matter this time.

Drake dropped down in his chair and pulled a file from a folder on the side of his desk. He tried to force himself to wrap up a few things before heading out to clean up the house and pack for the trip. It would have been so much better if Sicily had decided to come with him, but with the way things were now, there was no way.

"Whatever," he grumbled and leaned back in his chair. He needed to call someone to go check on her. She didn't need to clean up the mess with Martin on her own.

He pulled out his phone and called Jake, knowing the other man was solid gold in the way of helping out.

"Hey, buddy. What's up?" Jake's voice was upbeat and full of life.

"Sicily needs you and Kari to get to the shop. That punk-ass kid was there this morning and we figured out that he was the one who burned Judy's down. He set her up."

"I heard. You need us to go over there now? Is Martin still here?"

"Yeah. I beat his ass, so I'm sure the cops and ambulances are there. I had to jet."

"Why?"

Because I'm a monster with a record of killing, stealing, and fucking up entire cities.

"Because Sicily got pissed at me and forced me to leave. She's angry that I beat the kid's ass."

"I'm sure he deserved it."

"Of course he did. He had his hands on her and she was backed into a fucking corner." Drake took a long breath, trying to calm himself as his vision blurred. Anger beat against the inside of his chest and he knew he was going to explode soon if he didn't get into the weight room. He wasn't the kind of man who was okay with letting anyone or anything fuck with his world – least of all, his girl.

"Oh shit. That's not good. We'll head over there now. I'll text you when we have her and call you later."

"Thanks, Jake." Drake hung up the phone and dropped it on the desk as he let out a long groan. Maybe it would be better to go on a long run instead of going to the weight room. Autumn was incredible in Bar Harbor and it wasn't too terribly cold outside yet.

"This way I can get some exercise, let off some steam, and check on my girl without her knowing it." He stood and walked to the single standing locker that he had installed in his office for his gear. Tugging his ear-buds from a pile of wires, he tucked them into his ears, grabbed his phone, and headed for the door.

"Changed my mind. I'm going for a run," he called over his shoulder and walked out into the late fall afternoon.

The leaves had collected at the door again and all over the parking lot. There was nothing more breathtaking than the crimson, dark yellow, and burnt oranges that filled the scene before him. The large, colorful trees lined the narrow road that led up to the gym.

He took a quick right and moved more into the line of the forest, breathing in deeply and picking up his pace until he was running hard. Jake would kick his ass if he tried to talk the other man into something so aggressive, but for him... it was a walk in the park.

Forcing himself forward, his heart began to race and as he turned the corner to move toward town, the large lake opened up beside him.

Clarity was his for a minute as adrenaline pumped through him. Sicily was the woman he wanted beside him for the rest of his life. He didn't know much about her, but it was really irrelevant. He would find out any and everything simply because he wanted to be her rock, to understand her completely and be there for her, no matter what.

She didn't have the skeletons in her closet that he did, but if she were willing to dig through the dark spaces with him, one thing he could promise her was that he wouldn't lie about any of it. He wanted to put it all on display and let her search through anything she wanted to. If she could push past all that shit... he would propose to her in the spring the next year.

Knowing that Jake was going to propose to Kari at Christmas left him a little jealous, but willing to wait. There was no need to take away any of Jake's thunder. Drake could let them have their moment and then he would create a whole different one for him and his girl.

"God, please let her still be my girl. I'll give anything. Do anything. Just fix this for me?" He slowed a little as he reached the edge of the town square. The cop cars and ambulances were starting to pull away, which was a good thing. Drake moved behind a large tree and watched quietly as Sicily walked back into the shop.

Her long dark hair stole his attention, the remembrance of having his fingers wrapped around the silky strands almost undoing him. How badly he wished he could have reined in his temper just a little bit better with the situation from earlier. He hadn't meant to scare her.

She pressed her forehead to the glass door and closed her eyes.

Drake's heart broke in his chest at the sad expression on her face. She was devastatingly beautiful. His cock jerked in his workout shorts, his need to express himself sexually with her was all he could think about.

How close they'd come to making love the night before, but the situation with the fucking kid messed it up. Would he get another chance to hold her close and tell her how much she meant to him? To kiss her and memorize the thick, luscious curves of her feminine physique?

The need to run across the street and beg for forgiveness was only one of the many emotions running through him as he turned and ran toward the gym again. Nothing good could come out of him standing in the woods and watching her from a distance. If she saw him, she would freak out.

He made it back to the gym thirty minutes later, the run uphill having sufficiently kicked his hormones in the nuts. He was covered in sweat and mentally beat. Walking in, he nodded to Jasmine, who was up front watching the receptionist desk.

"I'm going to take a shower," he puffed out between deep breaths.

He half expected her to say that the cops had been by or had called and wanted to see him. The fact that Sicily hadn't turned him in said something – she cared about him. If she was held to the fire for the boy's condition he would quickly step in. There was no way she was taking the heat for his shit. Period.

Drake walked into the men's locker room and tugged off his T-shirt and shorts before slipping out of his shoes, socks, and underwear. He wanted a cold shower, and then he would call Jake to check on Sicily. He needed to stay hands-off until she contacted him. She had seen him at his worst, anger and aggression being the main characteristics that she'd attacked back at the shop.

He had fucked up royally, but it was her move. The ball was in her court.

The showers were empty and he grabbed the last one, which was the only one with a functional curtain. Most guys didn't give a shit about showering together in one large room, and normally he wouldn't either, but the raging hard-on he had would give the guys the wrong impression.

He turned on the cold water and stepped up to the spray, letting out a long groan at the relief that swept through him. There was nothing better than working up a sweat, and where he enjoyed working out, he would soon need to find another way to relieve his angst. Sicily being in his life was great for his libido, but awful for release.

He rolled a bar of soap between his fingers before putting it up and running his hands in quick succession over his cock, pulling harder each time he tugged at himself. He stifled a groan and pressed his back to the cold tile wall as he arched his hips, pressing his erection through his tight grasp.

The image of Sicily naked and leaning against the other wall seared through him. How badly he wanted to drop to his knees and spend hours with his tongue buried between her thighs. He hadn't let himself enjoy a woman like that in the last five years. If she was willing to give him another try, she'd have to force him to relent when he started to lap at her.

Nothing sounded better.

He picked up his pace and put his anger and rejection into the long, hard strokes he forced on himself. His body tightened as fire burst from his center and caused him to buckle. Drake reached out and touched the wall beside him as he gave himself over to the orgasm and whimpered her name over and over, praying like hell no one was in the locker room with him.

If so? Fuck it.

Drake washed off and got out of the shower, feeling better and more perverted than he had in a long time. It wasn't something he was ashamed of, but having to jack off instead of making love to a woman was low on his list of things to do again.

Time to get the girl back.

"You said you would wait until she called you." He walked into his office, praying silently that she'd called or texted. There was one unread text message waiting for him.

"Please let it be her. I'll do anything if it's just her."

The message was short and sweet, just like the girl who sent it.

Sicily: *I'm sorry for what I said today. I'm not used to high emotions. Forgive me. I'm going to Chicago with you unless you won't let me anymore. I need to know who you are if I plan to spend forever with you.*

Drake: *You sure you want to do that? Nothing good will come of you digging into my past. Today was a perfect example of that.*

Sicily: *What if I want to try and see the light in the darkness?*

Drake: *Suit yourself. I'll pick you up at 2 tomorrow from the shop. Be ready.*

CHAPTER TWENTY-TWO

Drake's response had come hours after Sicily first sent the message, which left her afternoon and evening ruined. She mulled around the house a while before taking a hot bath and going to bed early. She could pack in the morning before going into the shop for a while. It would hopefully calm her nerves a little.

After the fight with Drake, there was no telling how awkward the tension might be between the two of them for the long weekend. She hoped there was some way to push past it and find the budding heat that sparked between the two of them every time they were close.

Sicily woke on Friday morning to the sound of Lisa and Kari arguing about something. Checking the clock on her nightstand, she realized she was running late.

"Oh hell." She got up quickly and pulled on a pair of jeans and a sweater before working her hair into a ponytail and applying a little bit of make-up. Her hurried movements were namely due to needing to get to the shop on time, but even more so to find out what her two roommates were arguing about. She hadn't heard them get upset at each other once in the last two years.

Something must be up.

Sicily knelt down and zipped her winter boots before checking herself once in the mirror, and walking out toward the kitchen.

"I'll say it again. It's horrible advice. Period." Kari's tone was harsh and not fitting her bubbly personality at all.

"No. It. Isn't," Lisa growled back.

Sicily stopped at the edge of the kitchen and put her hands on her hips. "Wow. This is something I've never seen before. What the hell is going on?"

They both started yelling at once and Sicily lifted her hands. "One at a time. Kari?"

Lisa growled as Kari stuck out her tongue.

Sicily shook her head and walked toward the coffee pot. "This has to be good. You guys never fight."

Kari moved up beside her. "I told her that her advice to you about Chicago was horrible. You don't need to go to another city with someone you're unsure of."

"And I told her that he's Jake's fucking best friend. He's been around us for six months. If he were a serial killer, wouldn't we know it?"

Sicily turned and pinned them each with a stare. "What's Jake's take on it?"

"Glad you asked," Lisa started and stuck her tongue out at Kari. "He's all for it. He believes in Drake, but Kari has hang-ups with him."

"Which are valid." Kari turned toward Sicily. "He's got a mean streak. I'm not comfortable with you going out of town with him. What if something happens between you guys?"

"I understand." Sicily lifted her cup to her lips. "I will tell you that I honestly feel safer with him than anyone from my past. He is a bit aggressive, and watching him attack Martin yesterday scared the hell out of me, but never once did I feel like he might turn on me. He was protecting me."

"He was a bit out of control, Sicily. He put a teenage boy in the hospital." Kari narrowed her eyes.

"That boy set up Sicily as a criminal, blew up a building, and physically assaulted her at the shop. You're being ridiculous," Lisa scoffed and took a seat before turning her attention back to Sicily. "I don't think you have anything to be worried about."

"I don't like it. Period." Kari fell down into a chair next to Lisa. "People look great on the outside, but can be vicious monsters on the inside. Look at who Frank turned out to be."

Lisa's expression softened a little as Sicily leaned against the fridge.

"Oh, honey. I'm sorry about fighting with you. I just know that Drake is the guy for Sis. He's strong and bold, handsome, and such a fighter." Lisa reached out and rubbed Kari's arm.

"It's ultimately my decision, and where I love you both very much, I need to know if Drake and I have something between us. Part of making that call is me better understanding his past. If he is the guy I truly believe him to be, I'm all in."

"You're not worried at all?" Kari asked, sitting up straighter as her expression pleaded for attention.

"Are you worried that Jake is not the guy you think he is? The one he seems to be?" Sicily asked, moving to sit beside Kari.

"I guess at times I let that fear roar to life, but Jake's been incredible from day one." Kari shrugged.

"So has Drake. Just because he whooped some kid's ass who was touching Sicily doesn't mean he's not now. He's the one who got her name cleared and found evidence that she was innocent. Doesn't that count for something?" Lisa seemed to be pleading Drake's case awfully hard.

Why?

"But how? How did he get that information? Those clips?" Kari ran her fingers through her hair and let out a long sigh. "I'm just worried. I don't like it."

Sicily got up and squeezed Kari's shoulder before walking toward the hall. "I am, too, but for different reasons than you are. I'll text you guys nonstop, but I'm going. I've fallen for this guy, and before I destroy whatever might possibly be, I need to know that it's not worth saving."

"Good. Go get the bad boy. I mean... er... good guy." Lisa's voice echoed down the hall as Sicily smirked.

A quick packing job and she would be off to the shop. Violet was going to watch over everything while she was gone, and they were going to limit the hours for the shop. Nothing new would be made, but everything Sicily could bake that morning would be just fine to sell through the end of the day on Saturday.

"You sure you don't want me to cook?" Violet laughed and rubbed her fingers over her face, smearing flour on her pretty complexion.

Sicily laughed and finished replacing the cookies in the counter with the new ones she'd just pulled off the cooling rack.

"No, but thank you. You look like I've been forcing you to bake everything we have up here. Smart girl."

"Thank you. I swear it takes more effort to look busy than to just be busy." Violet turned as the door opened and Drake walked in.

His dark jeans hug low on his hips, the tight fitting black T-shirt only working to accentuate the thick muscles of his chest and abdomen.

"Girls..." He smiled at Violet and winked at Sicily. "You ready to head out?"

"Yeah. I just need to finish cleaning up in the back." Sicily let her eyes roam over him before returning to his face. She half expected the same cocky grin he had given her a hundred times before when he realized that she was checking him out.

He nodded and turned to Violet, giving nothing away in terms of his feelings.

It's going to be a long-ass weekend.

Sicily walked into the back and finished putting everything up before pulling out her phone and sending a group text that she was heading to the airport with Drake. She dropped the phone back in her purse and walked out to find him and Violet laughing about something.

"Okay. I'm all set." Sicily glanced toward Violet. "You going to be okay?"

"I sure am. I'll work hard to fatten these people up right." Her smile was radiant. Why wasn't Drake dating her? "Besides, I was just telling Drake that you guys could start the perfect scandal together. You feed them a load of pastries and then send them to us to work them off. Then we'll encourage them to stop by for a treat after their hard workouts."

Sicily smirked and walked toward Drake. "Scandalous."

"I quite like it." He shrugged and moved to the door, nodding toward her bag. "That all you're bringing?"

"Yep. I packed light. If I need something there, I'll just put it on a card." She shrugged and glanced back at Violet. "Thank you again. Call if you need me."

"Of course. Have a ton of fun and don't worry about a thing. I've got this." She smiled and waved as Sicily moved out into the chilly afternoon.

A black truck sat a few spots down from the shop, but Drake's bike was nowhere to be seen.

"Where's your bike?" Sicily turned and looked up at him as he stopped in front of her.

"It's locked up. I figured we needed to take the truck thanks to the bags. There's no way to balance the suitcases on the bike, silly girl." He smiled and nodded to the truck. "Hop in and we'll head to the airport. We can have a drink there or grab a bite to eat if you're hungry."

"Sounds good." She walked to her side and took a quick breath, hoping like hell that the calmness that sat between them would continue to hold everything together. She needed to apologize to him in person, but seeing that things were going good, it just didn't feel like the time.

Sicily climbed up in the truck and buckled in as Drake moved toward her. She stiffened as his fingers slid into the tightness of her ponytail, tilting her face toward him.

"I would never, ever, in a million years, hurt you. You know that, right?" His expression was serious, but his eyes were filled with warmth.

"I know that. I'm sorry about lashing out yesterday."

"Me too." He leaned in and pressed his lips to hers, his tongue brushing along hers as she opened her mouth to him.

Needing to feel more of him, she reached up and brushed her hand along his face as he continued to make love to her mouth. A groan left him that tore her insides up. For a minute, she didn't care about anything but having more of his skin against hers.

"More," she whispered and pulled him back down for another long kiss.

He broke it and smiled at her before nipping at her lips. "Fuck I've wanted one of those kisses since I had the last one."

"Good. I have plenty more for you where that one came from." Sicily released him and let out a sound of appreciation for the high level of lust racing through her.

"More kisses or something else?" He wagged his eyebrows and started to back the truck up.

"You'll have to wait and see." She chuckled and turned the hot air to point at her. "How long is the flight?"

"Couple hours, if I remember correctly."

"And D and Izzy are picking us up? Did I get that right?" Sicily tugged at her seatbelt and turned her attention toward the handsome devil in the seat next to her.

"Yeah. Izzy doesn't know I'm her brother, so please don't mention it."

"But she knows the truth about you not being dead... how? What does she think?"

"She thinks I'm D's brother and just got in too far into some shit a few years back. I think it's almost been five years since D helped me escape."

"Why is he still involved in all that stuff, Drake?" Sicily reached over and took his hand into hers.

"He loves it. He's a rough son-of-a-bitch and honestly, I think he'll be a Don one day."

"A Don? What's that?"

"The Godfather, or the head of the syndicate."

"We're talking old school mafia here? Like the movies?"

"Kind of. Sort of." Drake shrugged and squeezed her hand before releasing her and gripping the steering wheel. "I guess the real difference is when you get shot in the movies, you survive. It's not that way in the real world."

Sicily shivered and tried to put the idea of danger out of her mind. They'd been through enough shit over the last few weeks for her to never want to deal with deceit or lies again. Something told her they were headed into the middle of a world that simply survived on them. Was Kari right? Was Drake capable of slipping back into being that guy? Was he still that guy?

CHAPTER TWENTY THREE

Drake parked the truck at the airport and walked around, offering his hand to Sicily as she slipped out. The pretty little thing let out a soft yelp as she hit the ground. He reached out and slid his hands around her waist, pulling her flush against him as she glanced up.

"What are you doing?" A smile tugged at her mouth.

"Trying to figure out how to move us past what happened yesterday so that we can get back to working on whatever is happening between us." He leaned down and pressed a soft kiss to the side of her neck. "And hitting on you. Hard."

"Yes. I see that." She laughed and pushed at his chest. "It will work itself out. Let's go and do what you need to do together."

"Sounds good." He brushed a kiss by her ear. "Then I can hit on you?"

"Hit on me the whole time, please." She moved to the side of him and picked up her bag.

"Give me that, woman." He took the bag and laid it on top of his before locking the truck. He extended his hand to her. "Come on. I'll feel better when we're there. I haven't seen my brother in five years. It'll be weird as hell going back there."

"I'm just sorry that we're going back for this reason. Have you heard anything on your mother?" Sicily took his hand and he squeezed it softly, grateful for her warmth.

"No, but in my world, that's usually a good thing." He forced a smile and walked toward the elevators.

An older couple moved out as they moved in, the elderly man huffing as if he found something wrong with them.

Asshole. It wasn't a wonder that Sicily was nervous about being judged. Everyone who had eyes to see judged each other in some way or another. He had been the same as the rest of them before being replanted to a new location. He was far too grateful for another chance at life now.

"I need to come clean on something." Sicily's voice was tight with discomfort.

Drake forced himself not to interrupt her. He simply nodded, encouraging her to continue.

She glanced toward him as they walked into the airport. "My brother called a few weeks back when you and I first really started talking and he told me to steer clear of you. I guess he knows a little something about your last name."

Drake swallowed hard, hoping like hell her brother wasn't someone he'd dicked over in his past. "His last name is Moretti?"

"Yeah, I don't think you know him, but he sure knew you. I think part of the reason I blew up yesterday was because Johnny was so adamant about you being a really, really bad guy."

"Can't say I blame him. My family is revered in Chicago." He squeezed her hand and moved up to the ticket counter. "Hold that thought, okay?"

"Sure." Sicily moved in beside him and he slid an arm around her waist as he spoke with the ticketing agent. They got their tickets, checked in their bags, and walked to the gate as Drake picked the conversation back up.

"I'm not that same man, Sicily. I promise. I died to that a long time ago." He adjusted a small bag on his shoulder, and moved to sit down at a long row of open seats near their gate. "So, I need you to do something for me."

"What?" She sat down beside him and crossed her shapely legs.

Drake slid his hand over her thigh and rested his hand on her as she brushed her fingers up and down his. Her touch relaxed him in a way that left him thinking about a much needed nap.

"Tell your brother that you were mistaken. We don't need him involved in the mess I used to be in. If anyone finds out I'm alive, I'll have hell to pay. My father won't rest until he brings me back, and if Izzy or Marco find out that I'm their blood..." Drake shook his head and closed his eyes.

"Are they really part of a mafia?"

"*The* mafia, Sicily." Drake shifted and opened his eyes, trying hard to express the importance of his request. "It's a big fucking deal, baby. Please promise me you'll think about it. I don't want to ask you to lie to your brother. You guys seem close. I'm just not sure what else to do."

"I understand. I'll figure something out. I don't want to put Johnny in danger." She sucked her bottom lip into her mouth and glanced around before turning back to him. "Are we in danger?"

"I am. I always am." He rubbed her leg, wishing they were somewhere private for their conversation. "If you don't want to be a part of that, I totally get it. I tried to clean my shit up five years ago and honestly, it's working, but I never know if someone's going to show up on my doorstep to deliver death. Every time D calls I feel like that's it. It's all coming after me now."

"Wow. I would hate to have him call then."

"It's a double-edged sword, I guess. I care about him because he's my brother, but I don't know." I let my thoughts dive in deeper than I had in a while. "I think one of the things that I fear most is that one day he'll stop calling."

"Because he's angry at you for leaving him?" Sicily moved closer.

Drake moved his arm to rest on the chair behind her and leaned in, brushing his nose along hers. "Because he'll be dead.

His life is in danger all the time. I wish I could help, but I'm a coward. I can't live like that anymore."

"You're not a coward, Drake." Sicily's hand rubbed by his face and he leaned into it.

"Feels like it most days," he mumbled.

"Just because you're born into a family doesn't mean you're going to turn out like them. Being part of your family is just dangerous business." She pulled him down and kissed him softly. "Have you thought about changing your last name?"

"Yeah, but I'm a ghost, baby. I don't exist. If I try to change my name, it would put up a huge red flag."

"I see." She kissed him again, a soft sound of pleasure leaving her.

Drake pulled back and rolled his shoulders. "We're going to have to stop or I'm going to find one of those family bathrooms and show you how badly I want to express my feelings for you."

She laughed. "That sounds hot and yet not. Bathrooms are... eww."

The announcement over the loud speaker called for their flight to begin boarding. Drake stood and chuckled at the expression on her pretty face.

"Come on. No bathroom unless it's in a hot shower." He took her hand and pulled her up, giving her another quick kiss before moving toward the gate.

"This is for first class, Drake."

"I know, baby. My brother always goes in style. Should be fun."

"Fun, yes, but insanely expensive." Sicily moved in front of him as the flight attendant took her ticket.

"I'm not paying for it. D did."

"I need to pay him back for mine. I don't do freebies."

"Yeah. Good luck with that." Drake handed the woman his ticket and moved to take Sicily's hand again. "He's the devil in an angel's disguise."

"Sounds like you." She laughed.

"He's much better looking than me, so let me warn you now... No falling for him. I'd hate to kill my own brother over the girl who's stolen my heart."

She glanced over and he almost relented, ensuring her that he was kidding, but she took the conversation a different route.

"I've stolen your heart?" Her eyes filled with tears.

He pulled her into a side hug. "Yes, baby. I think I told you that the other night. It's the reason why I can put our fight behind me from last night. People who plan on working things out usually have to, you know... work things out."

She shook her head and wiped at her tears, shocking him with her beauty.

"Shit, it might be D I need to worry about. He loves a beautiful woman and Italian women are his favorite." A false sense of protection rolled over him and he forced it away. D was in love with Izzy to the point of it almost being comical. The two of them needed to let down their guards and have at each other. They had to be fucking. They were too attracted to each other not to.

Drake let the silence fall between them as they got on the plane and found their seats. He let Sicily get in first before putting their smaller bags in the overhead and sitting down next to her.

"I'm going to apologize in advance. I'm exhausted. I slept like shit last night because of everything. If I fall asleep..."

He cut her off. "I'll wake you up when we get there, baby. Just rest."

She leaned over and pressed a kiss to his shoulder before snuggling into him. The sweet smell of her perfume rolled over him and he turned and kissed the top of her head. How badly he wanted to tell her that he loved her, that she was the one, that he wanted forever, but it was too soon.

It was the romantic in him that fanned the hope of having love and raising a family one day. It seemed impossible a few years back, but now, sitting next to Sicily, that hope was coming back to life. He started to tell her how pretty she was, but the sound of her deep breathing stopped him.

"Damn... you weren't kidding." The plane pulled back a few minutes later and he closed his eyes, letting himself dive into fantasy after fantasy where the pretty girl next to him promised to be his forever.

"Baby." Drake kissed the top of Sicily's head, hoping to wake her as the plane pulled into the gate.

"Five more minutes. Please. I was almost to the good part," she mumbled.

He laughed and ran his hand down the side of her face. "I have lots of good parts in store for you. Come on, baby. Wake up. The plane has landed."

"Hm?" Sicily sat up and ran her hands down her hair as if trying to smooth it. "Where are we?"

"We're in Chicago." He stood up and got their bags down as she worked on waking up.

"Who's picking us up again?"

"Izzy and D. Come on, Sis. Get up and let's get off." He reached for her, helping her stand.

She was a little wobbly and Drake couldn't help but enjoy the sweet disposition that sat on her. She looked so fucking innocent. Why did he want to wreck that innocence more than anything else?

Because I'm an asshole.

"Sorry," she mumbled and moved in front of him.

He reached out and slid his hand around her waist as they walked off. "No need to apologize."

Lifting to his toes as they walked, he could see his brother and sister standing together, the two of them arguing about something. They looked as if they might jump each other in the middle of the airport.

"So typical," Drake muttered.

"What's that?" Sicily glanced up at him.

"D and Izzy are fighting. Get ready. They do a lot of that."

"Why? They don't like each other?"

"No." Drake laughed. "They love each other and neither of them will tell the other."

"Oh, hell. That's way worse." Sicily moved behind Drake as if she were nervous about meeting everyone.

"Hey!" Drake yelled and caught D's attention.

His brother let out a soft whoop and walked toward him, pulling him into a tight hug. "Fuck, I've missed you, little brother."

CHAPTER TWENTY-FOUR

If Drake was wickedly handsome, Demetri was a god. Sicily glanced up at him as he pulled Drake into a warm hug. His dark gaze moved across her as if he were trying to analyze her worth in one stare. He moved and Sicily took a step back.

She didn't belong there. Drake and D looked like models and Izzy was breathtaking.

A tall, long-legged vixen in black leather pants and a tight T-shirt extended her hand. Her sea-green eyes were filled with challenge and hardness, something that Sicily hadn't seen in a woman's expression in a long time. Her dark hair framed her perfect features, the girl giving the handsome men beside her a run for their money.

You look like a fucking idiot standing with them.

"You must be Sicily. I'm Izabella. Call me Izzy. They all do." She nodded back toward the boys as Drake and D continued to talk quickly as if they had a million things to catch up on.

Sicily smiled, forcing herself to calm down and play the part. "Nice to meet you."

"Let's grab your bags and we can take you guys to get something to eat. You hungry?" Izzy glanced down the length of Sicily's body. The girl's expression didn't give anything away, but Sicily cringed internally. She was being sized up, literally, and didn't have a chance of measuring up. She was twice as big as the gorgeous woman in front of her.

"D. Come meet my girl." Drake moved toward her and pulled her into a side hug. "Sis. This is Demetri and you've met Izzy."

"Nice to meet you." Sicily extended her hand, and was a little surprised when D took it and pressed his lips to it.

His dark hair and black eyes were stunning against his tanned skin. He was taller than Drake and yet just as cut from what she could tell. His button down grey shirt and slacks looked good on him, the man belonging on a GQ magazine.

"Hey. Back up, motherfucker." Drake pushed at D's chest as the older brother laughed.

"No worries, little brother. I love you too much to steal your girl." He glanced over to Izzy. "You ready?"

"Yep." Her response was tight-lipped. Whatever they were fighting about before Sicily showed up was obviously still jacking with the pretty girl.

"I'm starving. Let's get something to eat." Drake moved his arm off Sicily and grabbed her hand. She moved closer, needing to remind herself that she was his girl. He hadn't given Izzy a second glance, much less a first.

No wonder. She's his sister, idiot.

Sicily glanced toward the pretty girl as she walked through the terminal with her head up. She looked like the type of woman who owned everyone and everything. Too bad D looked like that exact same type. No wonder they fought all the time. They were both struggling to be on top.

Squeezing Drake's hand, Sicily realized that she was okay letting him lead. She wanted him to.

He glanced back and winked at her, smiling like he'd won the lottery.

She'd been so damned lonely not seeing her brothers for the last few months, but she could go back any time. Drake didn't have that option. How lonely his life must have been. What was he up against to have to have done some of the things he did? Was his father forcing him into leadership in the syndicate? Is that why he ran?

"What do you guys feel like?" D turned and pinned her with a stare.

She swallowed hard and ignored the feeling of being judged and found lacking. "I'm good with anything."

"Something in the next town over, preferably. All I need is to run into old friends." Drake shook his head and moved to the turnstile for their bags. D moved up to help him as Izzy took a seat beside Sicily.

"So Demetri tells me that you own your own bakery. That's pretty cool."

Is she making fun of me? Sicily glanced down at Izzy and tried to figure her out.

"Yeah. It's always been a dream of mine and since my degree is in culinary arts, it just worked out." Sicily shrugged and took a seat next to the bombshell.

Thank God I've lost some weight. If I had to sit here next to her a few weeks back... there would be no damn way.

"I love to cook. I just don't have much time to do it." Izzy turned her gaze from Sicily and toward the boys. "Drake's a good man."

"Yeah. He's great." Sicily sat back and forced herself to make conversation. "He says his brother is quite a great guy, too."

"D?" Izzy turned and let out a tight laugh. "He's an asshole at best. Don't let Drake sell you on that superhero bullshit."

Sicily chuckled, seeing right through the woman's facade. She was in love with the handsome guy, and the sad thing was, he probably knew it.

"I'm thinking pasta would be good for dinner. You?" Sicily turned her attention back to Drake, letting her eyes roll down his strong back and the perfect swell of his ass.

"Yeah. I love pasta. We eat it eight days a week at home." Izzy chuckled and stood up. "They seem to have the bags. Come on. We'll take you guys to the hotel after dinner."

The meal was great, but the company was awkward at best. Sicily let out a soft sigh when D dropped her and Drake off at the hotel. He rolled down the window as they got out of the car.

"I'll pick you up tomorrow at ten to go see momma. Be ready, okay? We have an hour window at the hospital. That's all I could pull off." D glanced from Drake to Sicily.

She nodded as if agreeing, though the conversation wasn't with her.

"Okay. Thanks, man. See you guys tomorrow." Drake turned and took Sicily's hand as the long black Lincoln in front of them drove off. "You okay? You were quiet at dinner."

"Yeah, I guess." Sicily shrugged and reached for her bag, pushing it into the hotel before Drake could grab it. She moved to the front desk, hoping that he would drop it. Explaining how she felt like the frog amongst royalty would just leave her looking like a puffed up brat. Spending her first full night with Drake wasn't going down like that. She could tuck away her insecurities and deal with them later.

"Drake DeMarco. It might be under Demetri." Drake moved up to the counter and gave her a look that said they weren't done with the conversation.

"Yes, sir. It seems to be under Demetri. Everything is paid for. Here's your key and your pass-code is twenty-six-twelve." The clerk looked up and smiled. "Someone will bring your bags up shortly. There is a full bar and stocked kitchenette as well. Enjoy, Mr. DeMarco."

"Thank you." Drake turned and took Sicily's hand. "Leave your bag here. It will be brought up."

"Are you sure?" She glanced around before giving up on understanding the way the hotel operated. "I'm not wearing this all weekend if our stuff gets lost."

"Why? You look incredible in it."

"Please. Izabella looks incredible. I look like..."

He stopped and pulled her toward him roughly. His fingers slid into her hair and he bent down, consuming her thoughts with the strong press of his lips to hers. His free hand slid over her hip and cupped her butt, pulling her closer to him.

She lifted up on her toes, wanting more from him. The feel of him pressed tightly to her left the world fading fast. They needed to get into the room. Spending the night exploring his body was something she'd been dreaming about since the day they met. She was finally at the point of not having to shove those thoughts and feelings away anymore.

Drake broke the kiss, licking at her lips before growling softly. "No more negative comments. You look like a woman I want to bury my face, my hands, my cock deep inside of. Do you think I would be attracted to an ugly or overweight woman?"

"No," Sicily whispered as a shiver ran down the length of her spine. His words drove into her, leaving her desperate for him to fulfill them.

"Good. Then hush about that shit. Izzy is my sister." He smiled. "Gross."

She laughed and walked to the elevator, trying to calm the sporadic beating of her heart. "Why do we need a pass-code to get to our room?"

"Because it's the penthouse. I told you my brother is a fucking showoff."

"I like him." Sicily wagged her eyebrows and let out a yelp as Drake dropped their bags and pushed her against the back wall of elevator as it closed.

"More than me?" He slid his hands down the sides of her thighs and pressed his hips forward, grinding against her a little.

"Will it get me into trouble if I say yes?" She smiled up at him, loving the attention that he gave her.

"I'll spank your naked ass and force you to rescind the comment."

"Then yes." She let out a deep laugh as he buried his face into the side of her neck and pretended to eat at her. "Stop. Fine. Stop. I like you better."

He moved back and pressed his nose to hers. "I like you only."

"Me too." Sicily tilted her head a little and brushed her lips by his. "Make love to me tonight."

"Can I fuck you first? I'll make love to you after I get rid of this incredible desire I've had to make you scream my name."

"Wow." She swallowed hard and kissed him again. "How long have you had this desire?"

"Since the night we painted your bakery." He kissed her again and rolled himself against her.

She groaned softly, her body aching for everything she knew he was capable of doing to her. "I don't want to wait any longer."

"Good. You don't have a choice anyway." The door opened and he bend down, scooping her up and walking to the large double doors at the end of the hall.

"Put me down, Drake. I weigh too much for this."

"That's two spankings so far for you, missy."

"I'm serious."

He put her down and unlocked the door before moving back toward her. She swatted at him and ran into the room, turning to face him as he stalked toward her.

"I've going to enjoy this so much."

"What? Enjoy what?" Sicily backed up as her pulse raced.

His sexy mouth turned up into a smile as he stopped in front of her. "Tasting and touching every part of you. Take your clothes off for me, baby. I want to watch you."

Sicily nodded and turned her back to him, pulling her shirt over her head and undoing her bra as sensually as she could manage with shaky hands.

He groaned as Sicily let out a short puff of air. She had to look like an idiot, but his soft sounds of appreciation drove her forward. She undid her pants and slid them down her thighs, bending over and internally cringing a little at having her ass in the air with nothing more than a thin strip of lace covering it.

"Oh God, yes." Drake moved closer and slid his hands over her rear before pulling her up and pressing himself to the back of her. His fingers moved up her ribs to cup her breasts as he kneaded them softly. The warmth of his breath on her neck caused her to shiver. "You have to be the most beautiful woman in the whole world. Do you hear me?"

She leaned back against him, rubbing her ass against the front of his jeans. "As long as you think so. That's all I want."

"Good girl." He licked at the side of her neck, one of his hands slipping from her breast and gliding down until he tucked his fingers inside her panties. He groaned again and she whimpered, jutting her hips out from instinct. "Mmmm... Sicily. Someone's needy and wet, baby."

"Me," she whispered, losing her train of thought. Nothing mattered but the sexy bastard behind her. Not who she was or what she thought of herself. Not who he had been or what would become of them. Only pleasure. The need for pleasure raged through her and forced her to stay with him in the moment.

His fingers slid down the slick skin of her sex, and he groaned against her ear as the pad of one of his fingers rimmed her entrance. "I want in here."

"Please?" She arched again, taking a little of him inside of her. White hot heat rolled across her and she closed her eyes, wanting to memorize the brilliance of his touch.

Drake moved back and turned her as she grumbled. He chuckled and leaned down, brushing his lips across hers. "Go get on your hands and knees on the bed. I want to taste you. I have imagined it a million times."

She glanced up, never having let a man do something so intimate to her before. "Drake..."

"Hush. Panties off and on your hands and knees. I'm going to take my time with you. Don't ask me not to." He slid his thumb over her bottom lip and took a shaky breath. "You're everything I've ever wanted. Did you know that?"

CHAPTER TWENTY-FIVE

He moved back and nodded to the bed, expecting her to follow his directives completely. She was a strong-willed woman, but when it came to the bedroom, he would be in charge, at least the first few times. He wanted to move from fucking to making love to her, but it wasn't going to happen for a while. He needed to prove himself to her, to bring her to climax over and over. The very thought of hearing her soft moans lift higher and higher sent a bolt of lightning straight to his groin.

He turned as she slid her panties off and crawled up on the bed. Her ass was bigger than most women he'd been with, but nothing turned him on more. He was done wasting time trying to win her over. The assumption was that she was his and wanted to be for a long time. She wouldn't have come on the trip otherwise. She trusted him and that meant the world to him.

Kneeling in front of the bed, he reached out and slid his hand over her ass, pressing down softly on her lower back. "Arch hard for me, baby. Stretch your hands out and lay your pretty face on the bed."

She moaned softly, but did as he said.

"So beautiful," he whispered, taking her in slowly as he massaged the curves of her ass with his fingers. Not willing to wait any longer, he licked his lips and moved forward, lapping at her once as she tensed. "Feel my hands on you, Sicily. Just relax and enjoy, sweet girl. Let me fuck you."

She mumbled something, but he ignored her, leaning in and taking his time to cover every inch of her swollen sex in his kisses. He bathed her with his tongue until her breathing hitched.

"Stop, Drake. I'm almost there."

"Good. Let me taste it." He pressed his mouth to her and sucked hard, flicking the tip of his tongue against her clit and positioning himself to let his thumb sink into her just above his face.

She screamed and he lit into her hard and fast, not willing to give up the ecstasy she was racing toward. Sicily pressed back on him, her body squeezing his thumb as the sweet flavor of her orgasm hit him. He growled again and moved his hand, taking her by the thighs and losing himself against her. She came again almost immediately, the feel of her body convulsing almost forcing him to join her. He'd been with a few women, but never anything like what he had with her. It was because love played a part in the moment.

I love her.

She moved forward, flattening herself to the bed and rocking against it as her ass bounced a little. Her soft moans mixed with whimpers were enough to undo him completely.

"God that was incredible." Drake patted her ass once and stood up, pulling his T-shirt over his back and getting rid of his jeans as quickly as he could. He crawled up on the bed and laid down across her back, tucking his cock between the soft cheeks of her ass. Tilting his hips, he lined himself up with the entrance to her body, pushing a little against it.

"I want more of that," she whispered and turned her face toward him as best she could.

"There's lots more where that came from. It's one of my favorite things to do."

She smiled and licked at her lips. "I need to return the favor."

"Not now you don't. I've got you all loosened up. Time to enjoy myself immensely." He kissed the side of her face.

"You want me back on my knees?" Her voice was soft and sweet.

"No. Stay where you are. I love feeling your skin against mine." He licked at her shoulder before pressing his teeth into her as his cock pressed against her tightness.

"Oh God," she groaned and turned away from him, pressing her forehead to the bed. "I haven't done this in forever."

"Good. I want to be all you remember when you think of making love." He pushed in farther, groaning as his cock pulsed with the need to come.

Not yet. Hold off as long as you can.

She arched her hips, lifting her ass and him a little into the air. He pressed in farther as his ability to maintain control snapped. He pushed up and moved to his knees before taking her perfect ass and lifting it a little more as he jerked back out, his need to thrust fast and hard taking control of everything.

She cried out and he slowed a little, rubbing his thumbs over her soft flesh. "Are you okay, baby? Too much?"

"It's so good, Drake. Don't stop. Please." She jerked back on him, and he growled loudly before rocking against her wetness.

The smell of their sex combined with the sound of their fucking urged him toward the cliff of orgasm. He glanced down at the beautiful woman spread out before him. His heart swelled inside of him. How could she ever want anything to do with him?

He would never be able to figure it out, but she did.

"Your thumb..." she groaned against the bed.

"What about it baby?" Drake rubbed his fingers over her again and glanced down to watch how well she took him inside of her.

"Put it in my ass. Please?"

He paused for a minute as her request caused his balls to tighten completely. He was going to come. "Yeah of course, baby. Anything."

He gripped her hip hard as he licked his thumb and pressed it to her ass, his focus on her and not on the raging need to release himself inside of her. She groaned loudly as her body tightened around his. She was coming again and he wasn't going to miss the chance to join her. He worked himself in and out of her until the world dissolved around him.

The guttural cry that left him shook him to his very core.

Mine. She's mine forever.

Drake woke the next morning wrapped around the beautiful woman in front of him. Memories of the night before had his cock on full alert and ready to replace his thumb. How badly he had wanted to offer the night before, but it seemed too much. He worked to get his arm out from underneath her, before getting out of the bed.

Stopping beside the bed, he glanced down at her and moved a long silky strand of her black hair off her shoulder. "I love you."

She didn't move, but seemed to be lost to deep sleep, which was a good thing. He wasn't sure she was ready to hear his true feelings seeing that they'd only been dating for a week or so. He'd been after her for six months though. His feeling spawned back at the beginning, not recently.

He walked to the bathroom and took a quick shower, washing the scent of her off of him. He lamented at the idea, but knew that she would give him another chance to coat himself in her. Smiling at the thought, he towel dried his hair and walked into the room, grabbing a pair of athletic shorts from his bag.

He worked to get them on before walking to the kitchen to start breakfast. There was anything someone could want in the fridge, and where oatmeal was his go-to breakfast most days of the week, this weekend he wanted to splurge with her.

Working quickly, he fried up bacon, made toast, and cooked a few eggs before walking to kneel beside the bed.

"Baby. You need to start moving around. I made us breakfast. Come eat with me and we'll get ready to go see my mother." He kissed the side of her face as she mumbled something about five more minutes. "Now, sexy girl."

She groaned and tossed a pillow at him as he walked back into the kitchen. "Remind me to never have you on my dodgeball team. Your aim is horrible."

He laughed and poured her a cup of coffee. The sound of her chuckling just behind him caused his heart to still. Turning, he extended the cup and let his eyes roam across the beauty of her curvaceous body as she stood on full display before him.

"You cooked bacon? I thought you didn't eat unhealthy crap." She smiled and moved toward him, lifting to her toes and kissing him softly.

He pressed himself against her and licked at her mouth before brushing his nose over her ear. "You're bad for my health. What can I say?"

"Well, I am a baker." She laughed and pulled back. "I'm taking a quick shower and then we'll eat. That okay?"

"Yep. We've got a microwave. Just make it fast or I'll be in there with you. The thought of taking you in the shower is..." He grunted.

"When my body's wet and covered in soap? I love sex in the shower." She walked into the bathroom and let out a yelp as he charged toward her playfully.

"That's it, you vixen. You're getting it."

He reached the close door about the time she locked it.

"We'll be late." She spoke through the door.

"Why don't I care about that?" He laughed and patted the door. "Hurry up and get back out here. I want more of you."

"You can have all of me. Forever."

Her words lingered around him as he walked back to the kitchen and paused by the stove. Forever. What an incredibly blissful thought.

D showed up right on time, which was very much his character. Drake got in the front seat with him as Sicily slipped into the back. After breakfast, the reality that he was going to have to say goodbye to his mother set in. Pain rolled through his chest as he turned to give his brother a pensive stare.

"You okay?" D asked and pulled out onto the busy Chicago streets.

"Yeah. I guess. How is she?"

"Not good." D turned and smiled toward the backseat. "My little brother treating you right? I'd hate to have a good reason to whoop his ass."

"He's everything I've ever wanted, and if you touch him... I'll whoop *your* ass."

Drake laughed and looked over his shoulder at the pretty girl in the backseat. His girl.

"She's from the streets of New York, Bro. You gotta watch out for her." Drake turned back to D as his older brother shook his head and chuckled.

"We have no more than an hour and if you can cut it shorter, that would be great. I can stay out in the hall with Sicily if you want me to or I can go in with you. Whatever you want."

"I want her with me, but just her. I need to ask for forgiveness." Drake shrugged and glanced out the window to watch the city go by. He'd grown up in the hood and loved every minute of it. The sexiness of a life on the run was enticing, but knowing that Sicily would never be down with the old him locked his thoughts up. To regain his pride by coming back would mean leaving the woman who'd stolen his heart. It wasn't a possibility. At least not anymore.

CHAPTER TWENTY-SIX

Sicily sat quietly in the backseat as her concern for Drake threatened to eat her insides. He was a hot mess over having to see his mother, and though he contained it well, she could sense his worry. The night before had been fucking hot and most likely put one of Lisa and Marc's sex sessions to shame, but she'd would never tell anyone that. She wasn't the kiss and tell type, though it would be fun to show her friends that she wasn't a complete prude.

The pulled up to the hospital and parked. Drake opened her door and helped her out before putting a vice grip hold on her hand.

He was sweating a little and his color was off.

She tugged at him and smiled sweetly as he glanced down. "It's going to be okay. I'm right here with you."

Drake stopped and leaned over, his fingers wrapping around her jaw as he pulled her up for a long kiss. His actions spoke volumes of his gratefulness for her being there. She forced herself to remain calm and steady, not wanting to let her own emotions at their budding relationship override the situation ahead of them.

They walked through the halls quickly, taking the stairs instead of the elevator. At the fourth floor, D pushed the door open and glanced at Drake. "Mom's in twenty-eight-fifteen. The cameras are off until eleven. Get in there and get out. I'll be watching from the nurse's station."

"Okay. Thanks, D." Drake took Sicily's hand and moved out into the hall. "Fuck me, I don't want to do this."

"You'll regret not doing it." Sicily glanced up at him and moved quickly, trying to keep up with his pace.

"I know, baby. I've regret too much already. I don't want to add this to the list." He pressed on the door and took a deep breath before releasing her hand.

Sicily walked in behind him and moved to stand beside him as he approached the bed. An older Sicilian woman lay under a handful of blankets, her skin pale and body visibly frail.

Drake's shoulders visibly stiffened as he reached out and touched the side of her face. "Momma?"

She opened her eyes and took a shaky breath. "Drake?"

"Yeah, it's me, mom. D brought me to see you." Drake leaned over and kissed her head as she mumbled something.

His mother's eyes moved toward Sicily, a smile starting to lift her chalky lips, but it seemed too much effort for her. "Who's this?"

Sicily moved up as Drake beckoned her. "This is my girlfriend, mom. She's a baker, like you were."

"Ah... she's beautiful." His mother turned her head a little. "Nice to meet you."

"You too, Mrs. DeMarco." Sicily reached out and took the woman's hand as tears filled her eyes.

"You know, Drake is the sweetest of my boys. He's the one who needs to be loved the deepest."

"Mom." Drake pulled up a chair and beckoned Sicily to come sit on the couch beside the bed.

"What? It's true." His mom started to chuckle, but coughs racked her thin frame.

"Hey. No more telling lies. Makes you laugh and then you cough." He reached out and brushed her hair back. "I wanted to come and tell you that I'm doing good. D got me set up in another city and I have my own business."

"Not killing people, right?"

Drake flinched and glanced to Sicily as she leaned back on the couch and crossed her arms.

"No, mom. Helping people. I own a gym."

"Oh, that's nice. That's why all that pudge is gone and now you've got big muscles." She reached out and brushed her hand over his arm. "You look so good. That pretty girl is lucky."

"I'm the lucky one." Drake glanced toward Sicily.

Pudge? Was Drake overweight when he was younger? Is that why he was so crazy about watching what he eats?

She tucked the killing thing away for a later conversation with him. Some part of her knew that the darkness in the past had to be taking lives, but what did that mean for them now? She had promised not to judge the man he was now based on the man he had been before, but if he was willing to kill people in the past... was he still willing to now?

The image of seeing him beat the hell out of Martin rolled over her and she tried to let it go. Now wasn't the time. He needed her to believe he was capable of overcoming his darker days, and in all honesty, she did.

"I love you," his mother whispered as the monitor beeped beside her.

Drake glanced up as Sicily watched him closely. "I love you, too, momma."

"Even though Joe knows your secret, you never have to be like him. Do you hear me?"

"Yes, ma'am."

"Don't let him into your life, Drake. He's a bastard and cares for no one."

"He cared for you, mom."

"Yes, and I wish I didn't return that feeling. Stay away from him and live this new life with your pretty girlfriend. Okay, baby?"

The monitor beeped again and Drake stood. "Of course, momma. I want Sicily to be my wife. We'll have a bunch of kids and I'll build her a big white house."

Panic rolled over Drake's features as he spoke softly, his ability to play off whatever was happening inside of him was incredible.

Sicily stood and walked toward him, laying her hand on his arm.

"Get a nurse. Now." He turned back to his mother as she smiled and closed her eyes.

"That's all I want for you, baby. A second chance." The monitor beeped again and flat-lined.

Sicily turned and ran from the room, plowing into D as horror washed over her. "Get a nurse. The monitor shows her flat-lining."

D turned and ran toward the nurses' station as Sicily stood at the door of the room, unsure of what to do.

Drake's mother seemed to have held on to see him one more time. Now that she had... she was gone. A soft sob left the man standing by her bed, his large shoulders rolling in as he covered his face and let out another one.

Sicily moved toward him and pulled him back away from the bed, wrapping him into her arms.

"I didn't get a chance to apologize. I needed to tell her all the things I'd done were in the past. I wanted her to see a new man in me." He glanced up as tears rolled down his handsome face.

Sicily's heart broke in half.

"She did, baby. She saw the man I see." Sicily pulled him close and he relaxed against her, the moment forever locked in her mind.

D helped get Drake to the car and drove them back to the hotel without more than a few words. He promised to call later that night. Sicily slid her arm around Drake's back as they walked into the hotel. He leaned down and kissed the top of her head.

"Thank you for staying with me today."

"Of course."

"About the killing stuff..." He pushed the button for the elevator.

"We can talk about that later, Drake." Sicily shook her head at him and moved into the elevator as it opened.

"No. I need to get it off my chest now." He turned and pulled her flush against him. Heavy emotion sat on him and she wanted to wipe it all away no matter what it took.

"Okay, but you've been through a lot."

"Yeah, but if I'm going to lose you... I'd rather it be now, so I know where I stand in life after this weekend." He bent down and kissed the side of her face. "I meant what I said to my momma, Sis. I want you forever."

Sicily nodded and moved back from him, reaching for his arm as the door opened. "Come on. Let's go to the room and watch TV and snuggle for the rest of the day."

"I'd like that." He walked with her into the room, rubbing her back softly. He locked the door, pulled off his shirt and moved toward her. "I was raised on the streets here. Being part of my family meant you joined up with the syndicate or you were gunned down. I had to protect myself and my siblings, which meant killing on occasion. I'm not like Izzy where I can take a gun to someone without personal cause or because of having to protect others, but I am a murderer."

"In self defense? Is that why you killed?" Sicily tried to see it from his point of view, but either way, killing someone was killing.

"Yes. Every time."

"How many times?" She reached for him, not really sure if she wanted to know the answer.

"Too many." He leaned down and kissed her. "I needed to ask my mother for forgiveness for that shit. She hated it. I didn't get a chance."

She'd already forgiven you, Drake. I could see it on her face."

"Can you forgive me?" He moved back as his features tightened.

"I'm not God, but I have no room to judge you. Let's move past this shit and we'll work through it little by little together while you build my big white house." She forced a smile.

He chuckled. "I said a white house. Nothing about big. Who's going to clean that mess?"

"Well, it ain't me. I cook, you clean." She pulled him down for a long kiss.

"Thank you for going with me today." He walked to the bed and beckoned her to join him. "Come here and let me hold you."

She didn't respond, but moved toward him, sinking down into his hold and tucking herself against his big, strong body. "Don't let go."

"I won't unless you ask me to, and then I'm still not sure I can."

She glanced up at him. "You were pudgy?"

He laughed. "I'm not opening that can of worms."

"What if I want you to?" She smiled and brushed her hand over his hip.

"Nothing you can say or do will force me to talk about my weight problems when I was a kid."

Sicily pushed him back and moved down to hover just above his waist as she licked her lips.

"Nothing will change your mind?" She nipped at the bulge of his cock through his jeans.

"I'll tell you anything you want to know. Just let me get my pants off first."

Sicily woke the next morning after a long night of snuggling and movie watching with Drake. Her body ached in all the right places from the passion of their sex. There was a million things she wanted to explore with him, but they had the rest of their lives. Her drive toward anal sex seemed to be something he was more than happy to explore with her. She smiled at the thought and reached for him on his side of the bed to find it empty.

A white note sat on his pillow and she got up, picking it up as trepidation rolled over her.

Baby,

Something's come up with D. I had him pick me up so I could help. Your flight is at two. I won't be home until Monday afternoon, but I'll see you then. Sorry I can't tell you more.

See you soon.

Drake

"What?" Sicily read the note three more times before trying to text him. He didn't answer, so she called, only to go to his full voicemail. What would be so damn important that he couldn't wake her up, kiss her and explain before leaving her to check out of the hotel on her own and fly home alone? She hated flying.

She finally gave up on trying to reach him and packed up her stuff, noticing that his was all gone. Had he changed his mind on being with her?

No the note said he would be home on Monday night.

Why not just wake her up? What an asinine thing to do to someone. She growled and got dressed, snagged a piece of toast from the kitchen, and walked to the lobby. After checking out, a valet took her to the airport and she checked in before texting Drake again.

Nothing.

What if she needed him? How was she going to get home from the airport? Was D more important than her? Yes, obviously.

Every negative emotion she could experience raced through her. By the time Lisa picked her up at the airport, she had unraveled all the good that had occurred over the weekend.

"Do you want to talk about it?" Lisa asked, reaching out and squeezing her hand.

"No. He's an asshole. Enough said."

Lisa started to respond, but Sicily pinned her with a glare.

"Yep. He's an asshole. I'm with you." Lisa nodded and turned her attention back to the front window.

Sicily felt the need to defend Drake, but she let it go. Whatever he was dealing with was far more important than her. Maybe that's how the rest of their lives would be together. She wasn't sure coming in second with him was going to work.

Maybe this was a mistake.

CHAPTER TWENTY-SEVEN

Drake reached out and squeezed his brother's shoulders as worry rolled over him. Not only had they lost their mother the day before, but someone took out Vivian Castaletta in a dark alley later that day. Demetri was pacing a whole in front of the fire place at his apartment.

"Hey. We'll figure out who did it, D." Drake moved his hands as D tugged away from him.

"No. I'll figure it out. This is my fucking problem. You can't get involved or all hell's going to break lose." He shrugged and slumped down into a chair as Drake's heart ached.

D was right. Getting involved in figuring out who killed Izzy's mother in cold blood wasn't something he could do. It would mean turning his back on his new life, including Sicily, which wasn't happening. He was too selfish of a bastard to let it.

"Did you tell the girl where you were going?" D snapped around, his eyes filled with hard emotion.

"No, D. I did as you told me to. I'm sure she's pissed, but I'll deal with that later." Drake let out a long sigh. "Tell me what I can do to help you."

"Call Izabella and tell her that I'm in love with her. Tell her to come over here and let me hold her. I know she's in pain, but..." He growled loudly and ran his fingers through his dark hair. "Fuck!"

"Stop being an idiot and just tell the girl. You lost momma yesterday and she lost hers too. Don't you think that both of you suffering such an incredible loss could bring you together completely?"

"Yeah, but is that what I really want for her? I'm stuck in this life, Drake. I'm praying that as she gets older she turns from it. I could tuck her away like I did you. She could find a good man to help her heal past all the shit she's seen. Fuck Joe for making her the enforcer of our syndicate. She's slutting herself out and hunting down the most horrible motherfuckers. All in the name of family." He let out another long sigh. "I don't know what to do."

"Just be there for her, D. That's all you can do. You can't make Izzy's decisions for her. She's a grown woman – and a vicious one, I might add."

D glanced up with a warning on his face. "Watch it."

"Fuck you. She's my sister. I'll say whatever the hell I want to." Drake lifted his eyebrow, ready to challenge his brother if necessary. He needed to let off some steam and though the timing wasn't right, it never was.

"You're right." D shrugged and glanced toward the clock. "I need to get back over to Joe's. Go back to your girl. Helping you find a real life is the only thing in my long life that I'm proud of."

Drake moved toward his brother, pulling him into a tight hug as D patted his back. "I'm sorry for taking you away from her. The damn day's mostly over."

"It's all right. I'll explain it to her."

"Protect her, Drake. You know as well as I do that not everything that's buried stays dead. One day things might shift. You ready if they do?"

"*When* they do?" Drake moved back and slid his hands into his jean pockets.

"Exactly."

"Not really, but who is prepared when their world blows up?"

"Not me. Obviously." D crossed his arms over his massive chest. "I'll give you a ride to the airport."

"Nah. Call me a cab. You need to get back over to the Castaletta Mansion where you belong. Just treat Izzy like a sister and love on her without expecting anything back in return." Drake walked toward the door, glancing over his shoulder. "Be safe, bro."

"Yeah. Love you." D nodded and picked up the phone.

"Same. Watch your back since I'm not here to do it."

All the flights were taken that night, which forced Drake to get the midday Monday flight. He slept in a chair at the airport, his back a wreck by the time he got back into Maine. In all of the insanity and worry he had forgotten to turn his phone back on. No wonder he hadn't gotten a call or text from Sicily. The fucking phone was dead.

He drove straight to his house and plugged it in before slipping into the shower. Sicily was probably worried sick. She would be pissed too, but he hoped he could talk her out of all of it. As long as he could see her, things would be fine.

After drying off and throwing on some gym clothes, Drake texted Sicily, not receiving a reply, which left him nervous. He called Jake, but the phone went to voicemail.

Kari was next on the roster. He thought about calling Lisa, but if Sicily was upset, Lisa would be a total bitch to deal with.

"This is Kari."

"Hey. It's Drake."

"Hey. Where have you been? Sicily has been worried to death." Kari's tone wasn't much better than he had expected Lisa's to be.

"I know. My brother needed me. I just need to find Sicily. Is she with you? She's not answering my calls."

"She's at home, or was. I have the bakery today, so I'm up here to give her one more day off. She was headed to the gym sometime today. Leaving her to fly home alone was a dick move, Drake."

"I know that. I didn't have a choice. I'll make it up to her. I promise."

"You better. Jake talks about how good of a guy you are. I'd love to see that on a regular basis."

Drake's shoulders stiffened with the truth that he hadn't been consistent at all as of late. Sicily probably didn't want anything to do with him. His life just didn't afford him the opportunity to be truthful, which forced him to look like a flake.

"I'm working on it. I love Sicily. I just need to tell her sooner than later."

"You love her?" Kari's voice softened a little.

"Of course I do. I started falling in love with her about the time my boy scored the prettiest reporter in town."

"You're pushing it." She laughed.

"Save me a few of the best cupcakes. I want to surprise Sicily."

"With her own cupcakes?"

"Hell yeah. She might have made them, but no one bakes better than my girl."

"I'll have them ready. Sweep her off her feet?"

"That's the plan."

CHAPTER TWENTY-EIGHT

Sicily pressed a cold rag to her face as she leaned over and studied herself in the mirror. Maybe Drake had left her in Chicago because he'd realized after losing his mother that his life was there. D needed him, which was obvious. Maybe having her and the gym wasn't enough?

"Let it go. He said he would be back today. Stop unwinding every good thing that's happened between you. The man cares for you and was talking about houses and babies to his dying mom." Sicily moved back and turned in the mirror, comparing herself to Izzy and coming up lacking – severely.

"I'm off to show a house. You sure you're okay?" Lisa poked her head into the bedroom and lifted her eyebrow at Sicily. "Get that cardigan off. You look great. Stop hiding behind your clothing."

"Do you think people can change? Like really stave off their pasts and become entirely new people?" Sicily turned and pressed her butt against the counter.

"God, I hope so. Otherwise Marc and I are in a world of trouble." Lisa smiled.

"How so?"

"We both would have chosen lust over love any day before meeting each other. Because of our love, we're totally different people. I would choose his love over the wildest night of hot sex anytime." Lisa shrugged.

"So it's not about having the willpower to change, but really loving someone so much that you have no option *but* to change. That love forces you to become different."

"Exactly. You're unwilling to disappoint the person you love and it forces healthy change upon you."

"Most of the time."

"Right." Lisa walked into the room and ran her hand down the side of Sicily's hair. "You okay?"

"Yeah. I think so. I just hope Drake comes back today."

"Me too. I have this feeling deep inside of me that the two of you are supposed to be together." Lisa smiled. "Corny, I realize. Don't tell anyone I said that shit."

"Mum's the word." Sicily smiled and picked up her phone, moving through all the messages from Drake. He had fucked up slipping out on her, but he had to have a good reason for it. How easy it would be to judge his actions without understanding more about him.

Maybe that was the way to get around pre-judging people. She would work to get to know them better and to understand where they were coming from. It might not always work, but with her and Drake it would be a great tactic. No one else would ever understand him, because they wouldn't be allowed access to peek behind the curtain, but she would be.

She texted him that she was headed to the gym. To meet her there.

Sicily swung by the bakery before going to the gym to check on Kari. The pretty reporter was in a great mood and taking pictures of several cakes when Sicily walked in.

"Oh. Hey. I didn't expect you. I thought you were going to the gym." Kari glanced up and moved her camera to rest on the counter beside her.

"I am. I just wanted to stop by and see you. Thanks for being such a good friend." Sicily walked toward her and pulled her into a warm hug.

"You bet. We're having dinner tonight, so get out of here and I'll meet you back there."

"We are? Who's cooking?"

"Um, the only chef in the house." Kari laughed. "You."

"Too funny. You need me to pick something up from the store?" Sicily tugged the strap of her purse up farther on her shoulder.

"Nope. Jake and I are going this afternoon after I close shut the shop. We'll meet you at home. If you see Drake, invite him to come."

"I thought you didn't like him much."

"I'm not sure I do, but I want to try and be open. I wouldn't have liked Jake much either if I hadn't put my need to judge him aside. Maybe Drake is the same." Kari leaned against the counter and let out a soft sigh. "Men."

Sicily laughed. "Everyone deserves a chance or two. Where would *we* be without second chances?"

"Not here." Kari smiled and nodded toward the door. "Get out of here. I got this. I'm going to run an ad in the paper next week highlighting some of my favorites in your shop."

"Have you been eating my profits?" Sicily winked and turned, walking toward the door.

"Just don't check the receipt book. Half this stuff is in my belly."

"You're fired," Sicily called over her shoulder and walked out into the early afternoon. Leaves blew around her feet and she decided to jog to the gym instead of driving. It wasn't more than a mile and a half and though it had started to get cold, it was beautiful outside.

She popped her trunk and deposited her bag into it before locking the car. She turned to jog up the long windy hill that led to Drake's business.

The need to see him sat heavy on her. She missed just being around him and knew she would be willing to forgive almost anything. The sadness of him losing his mother probably blinded his actions, and something had come up with D. She could talk to him about how to better handle her the next time, but bitching at him for rushing out to help his brother wasn't happening.

It would have been blissful to have Drake by her side as she buried her own mother, but she made it through the event alone. Tears burned her gaze as she thought about how much she missed her mom. A sense of warmth rushed across at the thought of her mom looking down from heaven and feeling pride where Sicily was concerned. She was healthy, happy, and successful. Now all she needed was her man beside her for the rest of her days, a few kids, and a *big* white house.

She chuckled and picked up her jog to a run, wanting to work up a sweat by the time she made it to the gym.

Her workout went quickly and Violet stopped by and chatted for a while. The other girl seemed amazed that Sicily had snagged Drake so fast.

"We met six months ago, so I'm not sure fast is the right word." Sicily stepped off the treadmill and took the rag Violet extended to her.

"Well, he's like a brother to all of us now, but we all tried for more with him when we first met him. He's just the full package deal, which is hard as hell to find in a small town like this."

"I can imagine. I wasn't looking, to be honest. I figured I would focus on my business and eventually the right man would show up. He just arrived early." Sicily smiled and glanced behind her. "I think one of the things I'm going to have to work on is not being jealous that he's around all these fit women all the time."

"You're fit, Sicily." Violet leaned against the nearest machine to her. "You're beautiful and so what if you have more curves than you want. Men like curves. It's something to remind them that you're feminine and a soft place to land. You're perfect and Drake believes that completely. I've seen the way he looks at you."

Heat rushed up Sicily's neck and coated her cheeks. "He makes me feel beautiful. I'm grateful for that."

"Well, you are. I'm going to get back to the front. I'll see you soon."

Sicily nodded and picked up her keys, realizing that her damn phone was in her purse back at the car. She would jog back down and text Drake to let him know to just meet her back at the house. She waved at Violet and walked out to find him leaning against his bike.

"Hey, sexy girl." He lifted a big strawberry cupcake to his lips and took a deep bite, mumbling around his mouthful. "There's only one thing sweeter than my girl's cooking..."

Sicily smiled and walked to him. "Don't be a pervert."

"Her heart." He set the box on the bike and pulled her to him, leaning down and kissing her passionately. The delicious flavor of strawberries and sugar rolled over her tongue.

She pulled back. "Damn. That *is* good. I haven't eaten any of my own stuff since I started feeling fat."

"Well, you're missing out." He licked at his lips. "Hey. I'm sorry about yesterday morning. D needed me."

"Everything okay?" Sicily slid her hands over his thick shoulders and looped her arms around his neck.

"No. Someone gunned down Izzy's mother in an alleyway."

"Mrs. Castaletta? Joe's wife?"

"Yeah." Drake looked over at the cupcakes. "Forgive me?"

"Of course, baby." She reached for the cupcake and took a small bite. "I never thought I would see the day when you would eat a sugary cupcake."

"Speaking of." He pulled something from his pocket and handed it to her, taking the cupcake and making quick work of it.

A younger version of Drake was in the photo with Demetri. He was a good hundred pounds overweight and had pie covering his little fat face. The smile on his lips was worth a million dollars, though. Sicily teared up and glanced toward him.

"Oh, my god. I love this."

"I hated it for a long time. Everyone made fun of me when I was a kid, but it's part of who I am, I guess. Being in the syndicate is part of me, too. I guess what I want more than anything is to have you accept me, regardless of the parts that make me up."

"I do. Nothing is going to change how I feel about you." Sicily pressed herself against him and looked up as one of her tears dripped down her cheek.

"Everyone has something, but who cares, right? I love you because you are you. Not because of your size or your baking or anything else. I love you because of your heart, and I don't think I would ever be able to love again if something happened to us."

Sicily lifted to her toes and kissed him hard, opening her mouth and brushing her tongue deep into his as he sucked on her offering. His fingers tightened on her, the powerful pull of his grasp leaving her assured of one thing. She was his.

He pulled back and licked at his mouth before giving her a cheeky grin. "There's only one thing I'll always judge you for."

"What's that?"

"Your cooking, woman. Too much sugar and butter in every fucking thing."

"I like the things I stick in my mouth to be sticky and sweet." She giggled as his eyes widened.

"That being said, I need you to bring home a vat of icing tonight. I have just the thing for you." He laughed deep in his chest and pulled her close. "Forever?"

"Forever. I love you, too."

EPILOGUE

Six Weeks Later

"Do we really need two cups of sugar in this pie? Can't we work on making our recipes a little healthier?" Drake glanced over at Sicily as they worked to wrap up their holiday baking. He had agreed to work the bakery with her from five in the morning to two in the afternoon, and then they would work at the gym together until the evening shift.

It was a lot of time around each other, but he couldn't seem to get enough of her. He'd asked her to move in with him, but she wasn't ready for that just yet. After Christmas... that's what she had promised. It was almost Thanksgiving and he was counting down the days.

"Yes, baby. Stop trying to jack with my recipes. Do you want me to go remove some of the bolts on your exercise machines?" She passed by him and swatted his ass – hard.

He groaned and turned to go after her as she yelped and ran for the back of the store. "If you remove a bolt, you could kill someone."

"If you don't add the sugar to a pecan pie, you can..."

"*Not* kill someone." Drake caught up to her and lifted her to sit on the pastry counter. He pulled her close and moved in between her legs. "You're killing me with your teasing today. I'm going to devour you tonight. Make you quiver and beg for more of me."

"You do that every night." She tugged at his T-shirt.

He pulled it over his head and pressed her back, running his hand up the center of her stomach and over her chest. "When is your brother coming into town?"

"Today. He should be at the airport at three."

Drake glanced at the clock on the wall. "Good. We have time for a quickie."

"Not here on the baking table. That's gross."

"You're right." He leaned over, picking her up and walking to the office as he gripped her butt. He pressed her to the wall by the recipe file and forced her to wrap her legs around him. "Here."

"Drake. You're corrupt."

"No, baby. I'm yours."

He leaned down and pressed a soft, wet kiss against her neck, wanting to lose himself in her.

The sound of the bell ringing above the door caused him to growl. "What now?"

Sicily slid down the front of him and smirked. "Go get your shirt and stop trying to seduce me in my shop."

"Our shop." He reminded her and walked back to the pastry room as warmth rushed around him. Hope was his again. Not only the hope of having a new life and a new existence, but in finding love for the first time and the last.

He swallowed his emotions and walked out into the bakery as Lisa, Marc, Kari, Jake, and Sicily turned. Stopping by the door, he took a shaky breath and realized that for the first time in his life, he wanted to be judged.

Judged as a brother who would walk through hell to offer assistance.

Judged as a friend who would never let any of them down.

Judged as a man who loved his woman – forever.

Judged as for who he could become, not who he had been.

Note from the author

Thank you so much for taking the time to read my second-chance story!! If you haven't read Jaded (Kari and Jake's story), or Justified (Lisa and Marc's story) make sure you grab those. The information is below. I had a blast putting together a novel for all 3 girls (Kari, Lisa & Sicily) in this trio. I know you picked up on the introduction of the Castaletta Syndicate, and Drake's brother Demetri DeMarco, which wasn't done by accident.

My Castaletta Mafia Syndicate Series is coming out later this year. It's been a brain child of mine for the last four to five years, so I'm crazy excited about it. Make sure you jump on my reader's list so you can see when it comes out if you're interested.

Again – thanks so much for picking up a copy of my work. I appreciate you and hope it gave you a break from reality!!

~ Ali

About the Author

Ali Parker is a contemporary romance writer who is looking to flood the market this year with lots of great, quick reads.

Want to know when Ali releases something new? Join her readers group! http://eepurl.com/bjCeBf

You can find her on Facebook (https://www.facebook.com/AliParkerAuthor).

See below for other books available by Ali!

BAITED

Rebecca Martin has achieved most things one might hope to by thirty. She is a successful business owner, drives a nice car and is wrapping up the details on a custom built home on the lake. The only thing she is missing is someone to share her accomplishments with.

One man has never been far from her thoughts – Kade McMillian, but his return to town after far too many years of chasing his dreams couldn't be more poorly timed.

With a younger man demanding Rebecca attention at the office, she has to decide between reconstructing a relationship from her past or diving in deep to something new and seemingly forbidden.

JADED

As a photographer for the *New York Post*, Kari Martin was used to seeing heartache and scandal up close. But one night at the club... her whole world changed.

Heartbroken and willing to call off her wedding, she decides a change is in order and moves from NYC to a small town in Maine, where the average age of the residents there is sixty (or thereabouts). She works to fit in perfectly, and tries like hell not to let anyone find out just how very jaded she's recently become over the lie called love.

Jake Isaac left Texas quite a few years ago; his heart torn from his chest, and his mind set on being a bachelor forever. Maine would welcome him, give him land to explore and a community to belong to. Getting a job as the coach of the local junior high and serving on the fire department kept him busy — and labeled him a hometown hero — but the truth of his damaged heart was forever hidden.

No one would ever know just how jaded he was about love. That is... until he meets Kari.

BILLIONAIRE ALPHA SERIES

Eight serials within the series.

Bethany had one more year of school left, and once again, poverty strikes hard. The only option would be to encourage her mother to marry her new boyfriend Kent, a billionaire tycoon in the world of accounting. Mom is more than happy to move the wedding date up, and Bethany's soon-to-be father is willing to pay for her schooling - on one condition.

She work for his firm as an intern throughout the next year. She agrees without hesitation, but little does she know that Kent's oldest son, Damon is the CFO. Dark features and a stare that would melt panties, he's everything one might imagine of a Billionaire's spoiled alpha son, her new boss. Her billionaire boss plays lots of games and though she hates herself for it, Bethany is more than yearning for the chance to fulfill His Needs.

BLOOD MONEY

Kate Jarrett has been around the block a few times, her life nothing more than a trail of failures. After her father dies she inherits the family bar, a place where she's accepted for who she is and loved for who she's not. Due to the location of her new establishment, a few friends from her past make themselves welcomed and death shows up at her door.

Jon Peterson is a seasoned officer for the NYPD, his record clean and eyes set on being the youngest captain in the history of the force. When his little brother Adam turns up dead at a bar in the seedy side of town, Jon's focus shifts. Is Kate involved in what happened to Adam or a pawn in a much larger game? Not interested in drama and hell-bent on justice mixed with revenge, Jon finds the one thing he never wanted – love.

Also by Ali Parker

Baited

Second Chance Romances

Jaded

Justified

Judged

Alpha Billionaire Series

His Needs

His Rules

His Way

His Place

His Demands

His Mark

His Offer

His Forever

Together Forever

Bad Money Series

Blood Money

Dirty Money

Forbidden Fruit Series

Forgotten Bodyguard